"Lynne, Why Are You Downplaying What's Happening Between Us?"

"I'm not," she protested. "But I don't have any claim—"

"Maybe I want you to," he said in a low, ferocious tone that caught her by surprise. And before she knew what was happening, he jerked her toward him and set his mouth on hers.

He kissed her with a stunning, single-minded intensity that rendered her too shocked to move. His lips dominated and devastated her pitiful defenses. Finally she put her hands up to his shoulders—to push him away?—but he only reached up with one hand and dragged her arm behind his head.

There was nothing tentative about his touch as he eased her onto the couch. He didn't say anything, just fanned the wildfire of desire deep inside her.

She couldn't speak, couldn't move, couldn't think, she could only lay there and feel as he removed her clothing.

It was then she wondered if a person could die of pleasure....

Dear Reader,

Animals have been an important part of my life since my childhood. In 2001 my family and I began raising guide dogs for Guiding Eyes for the Blind and subsequently came to know many guide-dog users. Brendan's story is my tribute to these friends, who deal gracefully and intelligently with daily challenges that I cannot even fathom.

Puppy raising has been an adventure that changed my entire family. We have lived the excitement of receiving eight-week-old puppies, the daily delight, occasional frustration and frequent amusement that occurred throughout the puppies' lives with us, and the heartbreak that we felt when it was time to let them go.

I strongly urge the dog lovers among you to consider puppy raising. Yes, it is difficult to say goodbye, but the joy and satisfaction of knowing the part you have played in offering someone independence and safety is an extraordinary feeling.

Wishing you warm, wriggly puppy snuggles (and an enjoyable read)!

Anne Marie Winston

ANNE MARIE
WINSTON

HOLIDAY
CONFESSIONS

Published by Silhouette Books
America's Publisher of Contemporary Romance

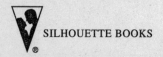 **SILHOUETTE BOOKS**

ISBN-13: 978-0-373-76764-9
ISBN-10:   0-373-76764-1

HOLIDAY CONFESSIONS

Visit Silhouette Books at www.eHarlequin.com

Printed in U.S.A.

ANNE MARIE WINSTON

RITA® Award finalist and bestselling author Anne Marie Winston loves babies she can give back when they cry, animals in all shapes and sizes and just about anything that blooms. When she's not writing, she's managing a house full of animals and teenagers, reading anything she can find and trying *not* to eat chocolate. She will dance at the slightest provocation and weeds her garden when she can't see the sun for the weeds anymore. You can learn more about Anne Marie's novels by visiting her Web site at www.annemariewinston.com.

With special thanks to my guide-dog-using friends
who patiently answered my questions, especially:
Sally Rosenthal and Boise,
Tony Edwards and Paragon,
And the whole Juno List gang.

And

in memory of every beloved guide
who will always live in his or her partner's heart.

One

Lynne DeVane was returning several more empty moving boxes from her new apartment to the hallway when she heard a loud crash and thud, followed by some very creative, vivid language. Whoa. She'd been a lot of places with a lot of jaded people but she'd never heard that particular combination of words before.

She dropped the boxes she was carrying and rushed through her open door into the hallway of the lovely old brick building in Gettysburg, Pennsylvania, where she'd just rented an apartment. Boxes were scattered everywhere around a man—a *large* man— she noted, who was just rising to his feet and dusting off his dark suit pants. A golden retriever stood close by, nosing at the man with apparent concern.

"Oh, Lord, I'm so sorry," she began.

"You should be." The man cut her off midsentence, his blue eyes on his dog rather than her. "The hallways aren't a repository for trash."

She was so stunned by his curt response that she didn't know what to say next. And before the right words came to her, the man groped for the frame of the open doorway directly opposite hers. "Feather, come." He didn't look back, but as she watched him fumble for a second with the doorknob, she felt concern rise.

"Hey, wait! Are you all right? Did you hit your head?"

Slowly, he turned to face her as the dog disappeared inside his home. "No, I did not hit my head. I banged the hell out of my knee and scraped my palm, but you don't have to worry about being sued."

"I—that wasn't it." She was taken aback by his abrupt manner. "You just looked as if you might be dizzy or disoriented and I was concerned."

"I'm fine." Now his voice sounded slightly weary. "Thank you for your concern."

He turned and found the doorknob again. But as he turned the knob and carefully moved forward, a realization struck her.

Her new neighbor was blind. Or, at the very least, significantly visually impaired.

The man vanished inside and the door closed with a definite *clunk*.

Well, cuss. That was hardly the way to get off on the right foot with your closest neighbor. She began to drag the offending boxes down the back stairs to the trash receptacles at the rear of the building, where she'd seen a cardboard recycling container. If she'd had any idea her neighbor couldn't see, she'd never have left boxes lying around in the hallway.

Even through her lingering chagrin, she remembered that he was extremely attractive, with dark, curly hair, a rough-hewn face with a square jaw and a deep cleft in his chin. The dog clearly had been anxious, and she wondered if it was a guide dog. But if it was, why hadn't it been guiding him? And if it wasn't, wouldn't he have been using a cane? Maybe she'd been wrong and he wasn't blind at all, just clumsy.

It didn't really matter. She owed him an apology. With cookies, she decided. Very few men could stay mad in the face of her grandmother's chocolate peanut-butter cookies, a family recipe bestowed on Lynne the day she graduated from high school. Neither of them could have guessed that it would be almost ten years before Lynne was able to eat those cookies again.

She hiked back up from the cardboard container and returned to her floor for a second trip. Maybe her neighbor would come out and she'd get another chance to apologize. But the door opposite hers was closed and it appeared that it was going to stay that way.

After the fourth trip she took a break and hung her grandmother's large mahogany-framed mirror above the sideboard in her dining area. She caught sight of her reflection as she stood back to admire it, and was momentarily taken aback by the stranger in the mirror.

The woman she saw was a slender, washed-out blonde with her hair twisted up in a messy knot. The woman she still subconsciously expected to see had a headful of layered, permed coppery hair and she was thin. Not just slender but really, really skinny. And she wouldn't be wearing ratty old jeans and a T-shirt. Instead she'd be in something unique from a top designer's fall collection.

More than a year had passed since she'd walked away from a major modeling career. Her timing was professional suicide. Even if she ever wanted to go back, she'd burned all her bridges completely. She'd just finished her first *Sports Illustrated* swimsuit edition when she'd made the decision. The only place to go from there had been up, but she'd opted out.

"But why?" her agent, Edwin, had asked in frustration. "You're the hottest thing since Elle MacPherson, honey. Your name could be bigger than anybody out there. Just think of it." He'd sketched a mock billboard in the air. "A'Lynne. Just a single name. The face of…Clinique, or Victoria's Secret, something major like that. How can you even consider quitting?"

"I'm not happy, Ed," she'd said quietly. And she wasn't. She was tired of hopping flights to God-knew-where for photo shoots in freezing-cold surf. She was tired of having to monitor every tiny bite she put in her mouth so that she didn't gain weight. She was sick of the casual hooking up and the partying that went on at so many of the functions she was required to attend.

But when one of the producers of the *SI* shoot had looked at her critically and said, "Girlie, you could stand to lose at least five pounds," something inside her had snapped. Enough was enough. She was already too thin for her almost six feet of height. And she wasn't even sure she remembered her real hair color. Like most of her co-workers, she sported a distinctive hairstyle and color as part of her public persona. Unlike many of them, though, she had yet to resort to bulimic strategies, binging and purging, to lose the necessary weight. Was she anorexic? She didn't think so. If she weren't modeling, she was pretty sure she wouldn't feel compelled to eat so very little.

But she wanted to find out.

"You might not be happy," Ed said, "but you're famous. And damned well paid. Who needs happiness when you're a millionaire?"

The thought that she might one day become that cynical was the scariest one of all. "I don't want to live like this anymore." Her voice grew stronger. "I *won't* live like this anymore. No more jobs. I'll finish what I'm contracted for, but then I'm done."

"But what in hell will you do?" Ed had asked, utterly perplexed. In his world, life was all about fame and wealth.

"Be happy," she'd said simply. "Be an everyday, ordinary person with everyday ordinary concerns and schedules. Eat what I like. Do volunteer work, go to church. Be someone who matters because of the good I do in the world, not someone who only matters because of how good the weirdest designs on the planet look on my body."

Yes, she'd definitely burned her bridges. She'd dropped the odd *A* that her mother had thought looked so sophisticated in front of plain old Lynne, and she'd begun using her real last name rather than her father's mother's maiden name. A'Lynne Frasier was dead, but Lynne DeVane was alive and well.

She'd moved back home to Virginia with her mother, gained back enough weight that she no longer looked as if she'd stepped out of a concentration camp and let her heavy mane of hair begin to grow back long and straight, although she wore it up and out of her face much of the time. With no makeup, her normal blond coloring made her forgettable enough that she'd managed, so far, to avoid recognition and the media harassment it would inevitably bring.

After a year, though, her sanity had demanded she find her own place to live. She'd decided on Gettysburg, just over an hour from her sister's home.

With luck, tucked away in a small town in the mountains of Pennsylvania, she would stay forgettable.

She crossed her fingers as she carried out yet another load of cardboard and stomped it flat before depositing it in the recycling container. If she didn't run into any hard-core *SI* fans, she thought she had a chance.

She was getting winded after the seventh trip so she walked around to the front and lowered herself to the front steps for a few minutes to enjoy the small-town atmosphere of her new home. Holy cow. She'd thought she was in decent shape, but those stairs seemed to be getting steeper with each climb. Lowering herself to the top step on the small brick porch outside the entryway, she took a couple of deep breaths. Under her breath she muttered, "Are those boxes cloning themselves? Surely I don't have that much junk."

"Am I going to fall over you or your stuff again?"

Startled by the deep voice, she whirled around. Her grumpy neighbor had just opened the entrance door. His left hand was gripping the handle of a leather harness now, but the dog in the harness wasn't the golden one she'd seen earlier. This dog was big and black and distinctly bulkier. The leather-covered metal handle, along with a leash attached to the dog's collar, was firmly gripped in his left hand. She'd been right when she'd suspected he was blind.

Jumping to her feet, she opened her mouth to apologize again. And then she noticed he was smiling. Belatedly she realized his tone hadn't been angry, but rather wryly amused.

"Sorry," she said. "Just taking a breather. Those stairs are starting to make me wish I'd added a few more miles to my morning run."

He chuckled. "Good thing it's not a high-rise."

She groaned. "Perish the thought. But if there was, there would be an elevator." She took a deep breath. "I really am sorry about the boxes earlier. I guess you noticed I moved them."

"I did." He smiled again, strong white teeth flashing, and she was mildly shocked by her instant reaction to the impish, bad-boy quality in the expression. It invited her to smile along with him, to share some unspoken joke. It also made him one of the sexiest men she'd ever met. And it was a heck of a contrast to his earlier behavior.

"I'm sorry, too," he said. "I'm usually not such a bad-tempered jerk. And I know better than to leave the apartment without my trusty eyes."

"Apology accepted," she said. She looked at his dog. "Did you dye your dog to match your clothes or something?"

His eyebrows rose and then he laughed. He inclined his head toward the dog standing patiently at his side. "This is Cedar, my guide. The dog with me at lunchtime was Feather, my retired guide. I was just going down for my mail."

"I thought if you weren't using a dog you needed

a cane." She didn't know what the protocol was for discussing a person's handicapping condition, but he'd already yelled at her once, so what was the worst that could happen?

He grinned sheepishly. "It's a hassle to harness the dog for such a short walk, so I don't usually bother. I should take my cane but the mailboxes are just at the bottom of the stairs and I have the wall and railing to hang on to the whole way, so I cheat." He extended his free right hand. "Brendan Reilly. I take it you're my new neighbor?"

"I am," she said. She placed her palm in his. "Lynne DeVane. It's nice to meet you." It was more than nice. His hand was large and warm and as his fingers closed firmly around hers, her breath caught for a moment at the leap of pleasure his touch produced deep within her. "And Cedar, too," she added belatedly.

Reluctantly, it seemed, he let her hand slide free. "Are you almost finished moving in?"

She nodded, then realized he couldn't see her. "Yes. Everything's in. And I only have about six more boxes to unpack."

"Only?" He shook his head, and she was struck by the naturalness of the movement. He hadn't been blind all his life; she'd bet on it. "That's six boxes too many for me."

"In a few more hours, they'll all be gone. And I can't wait!"

"If I were a really good guy, I'd offer to stay and help you unpack." He smiled again. "Sadly, I'm not that nice. I have to get back to work."

"Was this a lunch break?"

He nodded. "I came home to let Feather out and give her a little more attention. I'm an attorney with a law firm a few blocks from here."

"How convenient that it's so close."

"It's handy because I can get around without needing someone to drive me," he told her.

"I like it, too," she said. "I was looking for a place away from the city, but I wasn't quite ready to go totally rural, so this seemed just right."

"Which city?"

"New York. I used to live in a studio in Manhattan."

"Yikes. Those places aren't cheap."

"You sound as if you know that."

He nodded. "Columbia School of Law. I shared a place on the Upper West Side with three other law students and it was still pricey."

She nodded sympathetically, then remembered again that he couldn't see her. That was something she'd always taken for granted. It was a little shocking to realize how much of a role body language played in her interactions. "You can say that again. I didn't realize just how expensive it was until I started looking for something in Gettysburg. I like it much better here."

"It's a great little town," Brendan responded. "Any special reason you chose it?"

"Not really." She had no intention of telling anyone in her new life about her old one. "I came here in high school on a class trip and thought it was lovely, so I just decided to see if it was still as I remembered it. And it was, so I started hunting for a place."

"You're lucky to have found this. These apartments don't turn over often. The tenant before you was a bachelor who lived there for almost thirty years."

"Who knows?" she said lightly. "I might be here in thirty years myself." She cleared her throat. "Well, I won't keep you. It was nice to meet you."

"You, too," he responded. "Good luck with the rest of those boxes."

"I promise I won't leave them in the hallway," she said with a chuckle.

"If I'd had a guide with me like I should have, it wouldn't have mattered," he countered as he turned toward the street. "Have a good afternoon."

"Thanks." She almost lifted a hand before she caught herself.

"Cedar, forward." Brendan turned his attention from her to the dog.

She watched as he walked confidently away from her to the end of the block and headed toward the pretty little center square. She wondered how he'd lost his sight. He had an awful lot of the mannerisms of one who'd once been able to see, like the way he confidently extended his hand for a shake, or like the simple way he seemed to focus right on her face as he spoke. If she didn't know better, she'd have sworn he was looking right at her.

She thought again of the cookies she had planned to bake. She'd still make them, even though he seemed to have accepted her apology.

That evening Brendan was checking his e-mail when his doorbell rang. Feather and Cedar, lying on opposite sides of his chair in his study, both leaped to their feet, although neither of them barked. Cedar barreled toward the door, but Feather stayed with him, and he put a hand on her head as he stood, turned around and automatically negotiated his way across his office. "You're my good girl," he told her softly as they went down the hall and through the living room.

"Who is it?" he called as he reached the door. Cedar's broad tail thumped against the front of his right leg while Feather simply hovered near his left side.

"Lynne. Your neighbor."

She wouldn't have needed to add that. He'd remembered her name instantly. Not to mention the softness of her hand and her pleasantly husky voice.

Cut it out, Brendan. You're not interested.

It was a lot easier to tell himself that than it was to believe it. "Hi," he said, unlocking the dead bolt and pulling open the door. "I didn't expect to see you again today."

"I brought a peace offering."

He heard the sound of tinfoil rustling, and then an incredibly, amazingly wonderful smell assailed his nostrils.

"What is that?" he asked, inhaling deeply. "It smells heavenly."

"Chocolate peanut-butter cookies," she said. "My grandmother's recipe."

"You didn't need to do this," he said.

"I know." She paused for a moment and he'd bet his last nickel that she'd shrugged. "But I really am sorry for cluttering up the hallway, and besides, I needed a good excuse to make these."

He laughed. "If they taste as good as they smell, I can see why. Would you like to come in?"

"Oh, no, I—"

"Please," he said. "I fully intend to dig into these cookies right away and it would be nice to share them with someone who says something besides woof."

It was her turn to laugh. "In that case, I'd be delighted."

Brendan stepped aside and waited until he heard her pass through the doorway and move beyond it. Closing the door, he indicated the arrangement of easy chairs, couch and tables in his living room. "Please, sit down. Would you like a drink?"

"Do you have water or milk?" she asked. "Either of those would be fine."

"No milk," he said. "Are you an ice or no-ice person?"

"Ice, please."

What in the world had possessed him to invite her in? As he got a glass of water for each of them as well as a handful of napkins and returned to the living room, he decided it was the voice. He'd already decided that getting tight with the new neighbor could get sticky, but something about that sexy, low-pitched voice had completely overruled his better judgment. Setting his glass down, he reached for the coasters he kept on his coffee table and slipped one under each glass. "There."

Tinfoil rustled again and he realized she was removing the wrapping from the cookies. "Your dogs certainly are well behaved," she said. "When I was a child, we had a cocker spaniel who would eat anything left unattended."

"At least he wasn't a big dog."

She laughed, and the sound was a warm peal of music that made him smile in return. "Oh, high places didn't faze Ethel. That dog climbed onto chairs—and tables—and could leap right up onto the counter. Drove my mother wild."

He was used to hearing unusual names for dogs. But…"Ethel?"

"We had Lucy, too. But Ethel was the problem child."

He chuckled. "That's a polite way to phrase it."

"You have no idea," she said in a dry tone. "Are all guide dogs this well behaved?"

"For the most part." He nodded. "They're still only dogs, though. Just about the time I get to thinking my dog is perfect, he or she reminds me that there is no such animal."

"You spend a lot of time training them, though."

"We mostly just brush up on obedience on a regular basis and work on any specific commands we want to use. The puppy raisers are the ones who get the credit for the pleasant behavior."

"Puppy raisers?"

"The people who get them when they're little pups. They teach them basic obedience, they social-ize them around lots of people and other animals, and they teach them good house manners."

"Like not getting food off the table."

"Or out of the trash, or anywhere else they see it, which can be a real challenge, especially for a Labrador retriever. The dog learns not to chase cats around the house, not to jump up on people, not to get on the furniture—"

She cleared her throat. "Ah, I hate to tell you this, but there appears to be a large black dog lying smack in the middle of your love seat."

He laughed. "Don't ever tell anybody, please, or I'll get fifty lashes with a wet noodle."

"You wouldn't get in trouble for that?"

"No. Once we are partnered with a dog, that dog becomes ours. The only time a school might step in and remove a dog from a handler is if they suspect abuse. And I personally am not aware of anyone ever doing anything to warrant something like that."

"Feather doesn't get on the furniture?"

"Feather," he said, "is not about to leave my side. She's never been interested in sleeping on the couch or the bed."

"I noticed she went into the kitchen with you and came right back out when you did."

"Feather's having a hard time adjusting to retirement."

"Do they have to retire at a certain age? She still looks pretty chipper."

"She is pretty chipper," he said, "for a family pet. But she's almost ten and she's getting arthritis. She was starting to have trouble walking as much as I needed her to. And she was starting to hesitate."

"Hesitate?"

"Lose her confidence. She didn't want to cross the street, even when it was clear. One day she stopped in the middle of a crosswalk and wouldn't move. I still don't know if it was fear, if she was in pain or if she just lost focus. But that was the day I realized I was going to have to get a new guide."

"That must have been hard."

"Very." He still found it difficult to talk about, and he had to clear his throat. "We were partners for more than eight years. I hated it. Felt like I was pushing her aside. I'm sure that it felt that way to her." He sighed. "Some people keep their retired dogs, some let them go back to the person who raised them. Some are adopted by a family member or friend or someone approved by the training school. I thought it would be too hard to let her go. But now…now I'm not so sure." He cleared his throat. "Sorry. TMI, I'm sure."

"It's not too much information at all. I find it very interesting."

He heard the ice clink in her glass as she took a sip. "Have a cookie," she said after a moment, when he didn't go on. "They're always best when they're still warm."

"Twist my arm. Where are they?"

"On the coffee table. Ah, sort of to your right—"

"Think of the hands on a clock," he said. "If I am facing twelve, where would the plate be?"

"Are you in the middle of the clock or at the six?"

He had to grin. It was a legitimate question. "The middle."

"Two o'clock," she said promptly.

He reached out, gauging the distance down to the coffee table, and was gratified when his fingers encountered the edge of a plate. It had little ridges around the edge, and…there. He picked up a cookie and brought it to his nose. "I'm not sure I can bring myself to eat this. I might just sniff it for the rest of my life."

"I can give you the recipe," she pointed out. "It's not like you'll never see them again."

Instantly he could tell that she realized what she'd said. There was a short, horrified silence.

"Oh, cuss," she said with feeling. "I am so sorry. What a thoughtless comment."

"Cuss?" He was struggling not to laugh aloud. Most of the people he knew didn't bother to censor their language.

Again he suspected that she shrugged. Then she said, "It's a nice satisfying mix of consonants to mutter when I'm mad. I don't like to use—or hear—strong language."

"Cuss." He said it again. Kendra hadn't liked foul language, either. It was one of the little things he'd loved about her. "Works for me."

Thinking of his former fiancée made him realize that he hadn't thought of her in a long time.

"Anyway," Lynne said, "I was in the middle of a major apology."

"Unnecessary apology. It's just an expression like 'I see.' You don't have to censor your vocabulary."

He made a show of taking another bite of his cookie and miming pleasure, hoping to get past the awkward moment. Since he'd lost his sight, the only woman he'd gone out with was Kendra. And after they'd broken up, he'd stayed as far away from the dating scene as possible for a while. In recent years, he'd dated some, but it had never seemed right; something within him just hadn't been interested enough to pursue a relationship.

"I'm glad you like the cookies," she said. "Would you like to come over for dinner tomorrow night? There are more where these came from."

"Thank you, but no." His refusal was automatic. He might have almost mastered the art of eating without seeing his food, but he had a serious dread of making a fool of himself. "I have the dogs and—"

"You're welcome to bring them. A little dog hair is not going to ruin my home."

"You really don't have to do that." She felt obligated because she'd tripped him up in the hallway; he already could tell she was the kind of person who would take something like that to heart.

"I want to," she said. "I know virtually no one here. You can tell me about the town."

Well, hell. He could think it, even if he wasn't going to say it aloud. Without telling her an outright lie, there was no graceful way to get out of it. "All right. What time?"

"Is six-thirty okay?"

"Yes."

"Any special requests?"

"No spaghetti, please."

He could tell he'd startled her. Then she laughed. "I guess that is a bit of a problem food, isn't it? Okay. No spaghetti, I promise."

He couldn't place her accent. The way she'd said, "a bit of a problem" had sounded almost British. But every once in a while he thought he detected in her drawled syllables a hint of the South as well. Maybe tomorrow night he could steer the conversation in her direction. It would be a nice change from his usual routine of answering questions about his vision issues and his dog.

Lynne finally got the last packing box out of her new home. In just two days, after the furniture had arrived yesterday, she'd gotten most things in their proper places. Not many pictures on the walls or other personal decor, but that was something that would happen eventually.

The whole place needed a good vacuuming after she was done, and then she made another batch of cookies. She decided to make a chicken and bake some potatoes, and mixed up some honey-and-wheat bread dough. After she got it rising in the bread machine, she rinsed broccoli to steam later.

Cooking and baking still felt vaguely like forbidden fun. She'd spent almost ten years modeling, worrying about every extra ounce she gained, keeping her body at a weight far thinner than she would be naturally. Since she'd stopped, she'd gained nearly fifteen pounds. But she'd done it carefully and when she'd felt as if she looked more like a normal human being than a scarecrow in stilettos, she'd stopped and concentrated on maintaining that weight. It was ridiculously easy compared to the rigid diet she'd adhered to in the past.

As she soaked her aching body in a gloriously hot, soothing bath, she worked a cramp out of her calf, wincing as she kneaded the knotted muscle. She had to admit, even to herself, that she'd gotten a little carried away with the unpacking, cleaning and baking today. It would be pretty mortifying if she yawned in Brendan's face. Or even worse, if she fell asleep!

With that thought in mind, she drank a soda loaded with caffeine as she set the table a few minutes before six-thirty, then rushed into her bedroom to put her hair up again.

Her hand stilled as she realized what she was doing. Brendan couldn't see what she looked like! The realization was a surprisingly freeing thought. Tonight she would be judged solely on her character and conversation, on what she was like as a person. Her looks would never even enter into the mix.

It might be freeing, but it also was terrifying, she decided. What if she wasn't an interesting person?

Two

Brendan finished washing up the bowls from the dogs' dinner. He'd already taken each one out, but as he listened to the time, he realized he'd better get moving if he didn't want to be late to dinner with his new neighbor.

He was pretty sure his shirt and slacks from the office were still clean, but he wasn't taking any chances, so he headed into his bedroom to change. Clean pants. His fingers found pants hangers and he chose khakis rather than jeans and pulled out a brown belt, identified by the tiny Braille tag he'd used to label it.

He passed by the suits paired with dress shirts and matching ties on the metal hangers and felt the plastic ones that were his system for locating casual shirts. Better get a clean shirt, too. Showing up with an ink stain or food smeared on his collar wasn't the impression he wanted to make.

He was running his fingertips over the label that clued him in to color when his hand stilled on the knit shirt he'd chosen. Since when did he care about making an impression on a woman?

Quickly he finished dressing and called the dogs. He harnessed Cedar and put a leash on Feather. She tried repeatedly to shove her way between Cedar and him, and when he finally used a stern tone, she skulked behind him as if he'd beaten her with a stick.

"I'm sorry, girl," he told her as he stood in front of Lynne DeVane's door. "I'm doing the best I can to make this work."

"Make what work?" Lynne opened the door in time to hear his last comment.

He forced a laugh. "Sorry. I don't usually stand around talking to my dogs."

"Really?" Her tone held amusement.

He thought about it. "Okay, maybe I do."

"I don't blame you. They pay attention to what you're saying more than people do most of the time." The direction of her voice shifted and he realized she had stepped back so that he could enter. "Please come in and have a seat. But then you have to tell me what you were talking about."

As he entered her apartment, he told Cedar, "Find a chair."

"I didn't realize you taught them things like that," she said as Cedar took him across the room and he found a large wing chair with his outstretched hand.

"Good boy," he said to the dog. To Lynne, he said, "It isn't a formal command taught by the school, but when I first got Feather, another guide dog user suggested that it might be a useful command, along with things like, 'find the door.' Some people use specific commands to find a family member in a large store." He'd chosen finding a chair for the first thing he'd teach Cedar, and already his big black dog was catching on.

"How long have you had Cedar?"

"We just graduated from the training school two weeks ago."

"Oh, my," she said, clearly taken aback. "I assumed you'd worked together much longer than that."

He smiled. "He's a good dog. And having worked with one dog helps. When you get your first dog, both of you have to learn everything together. Speaking of which, where is Feather?" He stretched his hand down to his right side where he'd been trying to teach her to lie, but she wasn't there.

"Oh, I'm sorry," Lynne said. "I was petting her. Isn't that allowed?"

"No, it's fine unless a dog is working," he said. "She's probably enjoying the attention. Since I retired her and got Cedar, she's been getting more and more depressed."

"How can you tell?"

He shrugged. "She's not eating well. Sniffs her food and turns away. And she just seems kind of…lackluster. Dull. She used to be bouncy and her tail was always wagging. I could always tell because her whole body vibrates from the back end forward when that tail's going."

"It sounds funny to think of a dog suffering from depression, but I suppose it makes sense. Did you say you two worked together for eight years?"

"Yes. She just had her tenth birthday." He sighed. "I'm starting to think I should have let her go. A lot of times the original families who raised them as puppies will take them back again, but if not, the school has a waiting list of families who will adopt a retired guide."

"How could you give her up, though, after all that time together?"

She understood. Warmth spread through him. "Exactly. It's not easy for a blind person like me who lives alone to care for two dogs, but I just couldn't send her away. She's a part of my family."

"I can imagine," Lynne murmured. "I don't think I could do it, either." Her voice changed as she bent over and addressed his dog. "You're a beautiful girl, yes, you are. With a beautiful name." She laughed in delight.

"Let me guess. She rolled over on her back and has conned you into rubbing her belly."

"Oh, so you're a belly-rub slut," she said to the dog. "It's disappointing to hear that you'll do this for anybody."

He chuckled. "In a big way." He fondled Cedar's ears as a comfortable silence stretched.

"I apologize for grilling you," Lynne said. "You probably get really sick of people asking you questions about your dog or being blind."

He shrugged. "You get used to it. It drove me crazy the first year or so, but it comes with the territory."

"So you haven't always been blind." It was more a statement than a question. "I thought from some of your mannerisms that you had been able to see once."

"I was sighted until I was twenty-one. While I was in college, I fell over a balcony railing at a frat party and landed mostly on my head."

"Holy cow. You're lucky you survived."

He nodded. "Very."

"A frat party," she said reflectively. "I never went to college. Are those as wild and debauched as I've heard?"

He grinned. "I've been to a few that fit that description. But I hadn't been drinking that night. A guy behind me tripped, and it was just sheer lousy luck that he plowed into me."

"No kidding," she said with feeling. "Did you know right away that you were blind?"

"Not right away." He hesitated as the memories of those early days in the hospital welled up. Kendra had been with him when he'd asked the doctor about his vision.

"Let's change the subject," Lynne said. "I think it's your turn to ask the questions."

He realized he'd been silent too long, and he mentally smacked himself. He really *was* out of touch with socializing. Entertaining clients was a lot different from dating. Even if this wasn't really a date. "Sorry. It brings back a lot of memories. It was…a time of enormous change for me."

"I can imagine," she murmured.

He decided to take her up on her offer. "What kind of work do you do?"

He felt a subtle change in the room, a tension that surprised him. He'd expected that to be a fairly safe question.

"I'm not working right now," she said. "But I have a couple of interviews this week, so I'm hoping to have an answer to that question soon."

"Okay," he said. She'd probably just lost a job, and since that often happened under difficult circumstances even to the best of people, she might feel embarrassed or humiliated. "Let me rephrase that. What kind of work would you like to do?"

"My interviews are at a preschool and at an elementary school as an aide," she responded. "But what I'd really like to do is go to college and learn to teach."

"What age would you prefer?"

"I'm not sure," she admitted. "I enjoy little kids,

but I honestly don't know enough about older children or teens to know whether or not I'd also like those age groups. Hence the job choices."

"So you haven't worked with children in the past?"

"No." He heard her stand. "Can I get you something to drink?"

"Iced tea?" he asked.

"I happen to have some. Sugar or lemon?"

"Just lemon, please." He listened to the pad of her feet across the room and into what sounded like her kitchen, judging from the tile floor onto which she walked. Her place appeared to be laid out just like his, except with the floor plan reversed. The jingle of Feather's tags alerted him that she had followed Lynne.

Was it his imagination or had his hostess become uncomfortable the moment he'd asked about her past? She'd leaped into action right after that, and she certainly hadn't volunteered any information about what she'd been doing before she moved to Gettysburg.

He heard the clink of ice cubes, and a minute later Lynne returned with his tea.

"Is there anyplace in particular you would like me to put this?" she asked.

"Is there a table near me?"

"There's an end table on the right side of your chair."

"You can set it down there."

He heard her moving toward him, and as the glass

settled on the table, a whiff of clean, womanly fragrance enveloped him. She was close.

How tall was she? He thought she was probably pretty tall for a woman because her voice didn't sound as if it was coming from miles below him when she was facing him.

"There," she said. "It's toward the front of the table on the corner closest to you."

He reached out and lightly followed the lip of the table forward until his hand encountered the cool, smooth glass. "Thank you."

"You're welcome. Dinner will be ready in a little bit. I played it safe and baked a chicken."

"I like baked chicken. Any potatoes?" he asked hopefully.

"Also baked. Double-stuffed."

"The kind with sour cream and cheese all mashed up with the potato and then put back in the shell?"

She laughed. "The skin, not the shell."

"Whatever." He dismissed semantics. "Sounds great, especially to someone who eats most of his food out of take-out containers or microwave dishes."

"I guess cooking is difficult," she said tentatively.

He laughed, picking up his tea and taking a sip. "I know another blind guy who's a fabulous cook. He's a partial, which makes it a little easier for him—"

"A partial?"

"A person who still has some vision, although it's usually pretty limited. Some partials have more vision in one eye than the other, some have vision in certain quadrants of their field of vision. I have no vision, so I'm a total."

"I'm sorry I interrupted. You were talking about your friend who cooks."

He smiled. "No problem. I was only going to say that even when I could see, it wasn't at the top of my list of fun stuff to do."

"I always enjoyed cooking, even when I was a little girl. I haven't done much of it in a long time, though."

It seemed like an odd statement, and he wished he could have seen her face. "Life too busy?"

"Something like that," she murmured. "Have you always lived here?"

He recognized an about-face in conversational direction when he heard one. "No. I grew up in rural Pennsylvania, out near Pittsburgh. How about you?"

"A teeny little town called Barboursville in Virginia."

"Is that anywhere near Williamsburg?"

"No. It's above Richmond. Why?"

"One of the partners in my firm went to college at William & Mary. We were high school buddies so I was down there to visit a couple of times."

"I forgot you told me you were with a law practice."

He nodded. "Yes. Brinkmen & Brinkmen. Our offices are right on Baltimore Street downtown."

"I've seen them. It's a very charming little town."

"And convenient, too."

"Convenient?"

"Easy for me to get around independently."

"Oh, right." She paused. "I guess I didn't think about that. You don't drive, so you have to have at least basic services within walking distance." She sounded as if she were talking more to herself than him.

"A lot of vision-impaired people live in large urban areas," he said, "because things are so much more convenient, and there's public transportation close at hand."

"Didn't think about that, either," she admitted.

"Proximity to the things I need was one of the major attractions about Gettysburg. Main Street has a thriving business area thanks to the college and the tourists, so banking and doctors and dry cleaners are all within walking distance. And there's a grocery store and a pharmacy, too, and some great restaurants."

"Do you ever go over to the college?"

He nodded. "A lot of their music and theater performances, as well as the occasional guest lecture are open to the public."

"Oh, good," she said, sounding delighted. "I love music."

"Do you play an instrument?"

"No. I played piano when I was a kid. It's something I've always wanted to take up again." Her voice sounded wistful.

"Maybe this is your chance," he said.

"Maybe it is. So what else does one do in Gettysburg?"

"Well," he said, "I hope you enjoy Civil War history."

She laughed. "Guilty. It was one of the things that drew me to the area. I want to learn more about the battlefield and the whole war."

"I doubt you'll have any trouble."

She chuckled. "What else?"

"The usual things," he said, "with an extra focus on history, perhaps. There's a Community Concert Association, a library, a humane society, performing groups, a bunch of churches, business and civic organizations, stuff like that. If you want to get involved, I guarantee you'll be welcomed with open arms."

"I've never done any volunteer work. I wouldn't know what to do." Her tone was doubtful.

"You don't need prior experience." He felt like a cheerleader, and he wondered why she had so little self-confidence. "If you go to a meeting or two or join a church, it won't be long before you're being asked to help with things."

"That would be nice." He heard her rise. "Dinner should be about ready. Why don't we go to the table now?"

Dinner was delicious and the conversation easy and inconsequential. They lingered for more than an hour, sharing coffee and cookies after the meal. Finally, he remembered that he had an extremely early morning the following day. He was just rising when her telephone rang.

"Excuse me." She stepped away from him and he heard her pick up a handset. "I'd better take this," she said, apparently having looked at the Caller Identification screen. "Hello?" Her voice sounded cautious and cool and although he knew it was rude to eavesdrop, he could hardly help hearing her side of the conversation.

"Hello, Daddy." Her voice lilted with a pleasure he would have given a lot to have aimed at him. "How are you?… Yes. Yes. I know I haven't. Oh." The lilt flattened with what sounded a lot like disappointment. "…I see. When?… Congratulations. No, I don't believe I'm going to have the time…. I'd rather you didn't. No…maybe at Christmas. I'll have to see if I can get away." Her voice had taken on a bleak, distant tone. "Well, thank you for calling. I'm entertaining so I can't chat."

She concluded the conversation with speed and an affectionate word of farewell that sounded more rote than genuine.

As she set the handset back in the receiver, he hastily reached for another cookie so she wouldn't think he'd been listening to her conversation. Even if he had.

She returned to her seat silently.

After a moment that seemed to stretch for a long, awkward time, he finally said, "Is something the matter?"

"My father." She hesitated, then said, "My father's getting married again."

"I'm sorry," he said cautiously. "I take it that's bad news?"

She drew in a shuddering breath and he realized she was near tears. Somewhere down to his left, Feather whined, and he heard her get to her feet.

A moment later Lynne gave a shaky laugh. "Thanks, girl." To him she said, "Your dog just gave me a kiss. I think she's worried about me."

"She's not the only one." Without thinking he reached out and placed his hand over the arm he'd heard her lay on the table, then slipped his palm down until he was covering her hand.

He felt her lay her other hand atop his and gently squeeze, then she slid both hands away. "I appreciate your concern, but I'm all right," she said quietly. "I should be used to it by now."

"Used to…your father not being married to your mother anymore?" Maybe her father had had a case of the forty-something itch and had scratched it with a divorce and a younger woman, not necessarily in that order. Lord knew he saw enough of that in his business.

To his surprise, she heaved an unladylike snort. "My parents were divorced when I was two," she told him. "This lucky lady will be my father's sixth wife."

He knew his eyebrows rose, and he couldn't hide his surprise. "Whoa. That's…a lot of wives."

To his relief she laughed. "And that's the understatement of the decade." She took a sip of her coffee, and the cup clinked as she set it down. "Sorry to let that intrude into our evening. He always manages to shock me when he tells me about his newest relationship, although I don't know why." She cleared her throat. "Feather was very sweet. Has she always reacted to human distress like that?"

He shook his head. "Not in general, although when she senses I'm upset she does the same thing. But as far as I know, you're the only other person to receive the honor of a sloppy canine kiss."

"I liked it," she said. She rose from the table. "Would you like some more cookies to take with you?"

"Maybe just a few," he said. "I have to confess that the first batch you gave me is gone already."

"Better you than me," she said. "I—"

A loud growl interrupted what she'd been about to say.

"Feather!" He looked in the direction of the sound.

"What's wrong?" asked Lynne.

He sighed. "I guess she took exception to something Cedar did or maybe just the way he looked at her. She's not handling being supplanted gracefully at all." He called his guide to him, hearing the jingle of Cedar's tags as he rose from where he'd been lying beneath the table.

"Poor girl," Lynne said. "I can imagine how she must feel." Her voice sounded lower and faraway, and he realized she had bent over and was hugging Feather. "It's no fun being replaced, is it?"

"And watching me walk out the door with him

each morning is hard on her." He shook his head, thinking that having a father getting married for the sixth time, Lynne knew a fair amount about being replaced in someone's affections. "Like I said, I really don't want to part with her, but if she would be happier somewhere else, it isn't fair of me to keep her."

He rose and found Cedar's harness. It still felt new and odd after the softness of the leather on Feather's old one.

Lynne moved ahead of him to the door, and he called Feather to come along. He hadn't bothered with a leash since they were just going across the hallway.

But he didn't hear the familiar jingling of her tags.

"Feather, come."

Nothing.

"What is she doing?" he finally asked Lynne. There had been a time when he'd have hated needing to ask someone to describe what he couldn't see, but he'd passed that point years ago. More or less. He ignored the twinge of annoyance he felt.

"Ah, she's still lying on the rug in the kitchen," Lynne said.

He tried again. "Feather, come." But he still heard nothing. "Dog," he muttered beneath his breath, "if I have to come over there and get you, it isn't going to be pretty."

Lynne sounded as if she were trying not to laugh. "She's welcome to stay."

Stay? "No, thanks," he said. "What an imposition

that would be. Come to dinner, leave a dog behind for you to take care of."

"I wouldn't mind, honestly." Her voice was soft.

With sudden clarity, he remembered the phone call she'd just received. She'd been pretty upset by it, no matter how well she'd pretended to recover. And Feather had comforted her. Maybe...

"All right," he said before he could think about it too much more. "If you really want her, she can stay. You two can have a sleep-over." He turned back in the direction of her kitchen. "But she still needs to come when I call her. Feather! Come!" He used the I-am-not-kidding tone he rarely employed, and this time he heard her as she heaved herself to her feet, lazily stretched and shook and finally strolled toward him.

"Smart-aleck," he told her when she reached his side. He grabbed her collar as she attempted to worm her way between Cedar and him. "No, girl. Sorry." He knelt, laying an arm across her soft back. "Would you like to stay with Lynne tonight?"

"You could get her when you come home from work tomorrow," Lynne said hopefully. "I have an interview at one o'clock but I don't expect to be gone more than an hour, if that. She wouldn't be alone all day."

And neither would Lynne, he thought, reading between the lines. "Works for me," he said, "if you're sure that's not a problem."

"Not at all." The lilt in her voice told him she was being truthful. "I'd love the company."

"Okay." He snuggled his old dog for a moment, then rose and picked up Cedar's harness. "We'll see how she acts when I walk out the door."

He gave the forward command as Lynne opened her front door, and Cedar led him straight across the hall to stop in front of his own door. "What did she do?" he asked.

"She went back to the kitchen and lay down on the rug again."

He chuckled, although he felt vaguely hurt. "Traitor." He extended his right hand, realizing that he was anticipating the touch of hers just a little too much. "Thank you for dinner. And again, for the cookies."

She placed her hand in his, and the physical awareness that had simmered all through dinner hit him squarely in the solar plexus.

Lynne stilled as their hands clasped. Stilled completely, as if she were frozen. His body began to stir to life at the touch of her soft flesh. Her hand was small and delicate, nearly swallowed by his much-larger one, and he simply held it, unable to make himself release her. Slowly he rubbed his thumb over the back of her hand and heard her suck in her breath sharply. Satisfaction rushed through him. She felt it, too.

What the hell do you think you're doing? You're not interested in a relationship.

Chemistry, he assured himself. That's all it was. It didn't mean anything. And yet—he still held her hand clasped in his.

Her telephone rang, shrill in the silence that had fallen between them. He felt her hand jump and let her slide it from his. "That would be my sister," she said, "calling to commiserate. I guess Dad just told her, too."

He followed her lead, not acknowledging the moment that had passed, although he was still acutely aware of her. "I'll let you get that," he said. "How about we meet in the hallway at ten-thirty to take them out for the night? I'll teach you her commands then."

"All right." She touched his arm briefly, hastily. "Thank you for coming over. See you in a bit." She dashed back into her own apartment as the phone rang again, and he heard her door close.

Three

"Feather, do you want to go out?"

Lynne slipped on a light jacket, then picked up the soft leather leash that she'd found hanging on her door. His dog trotted to her, tail happily wagging. Her whole back end was wagging, Lynne realized, and she smiled as she clipped the leash to the D-ring on Feather's collar. "You're a sweet girl, did you know that?"

If a dog could grin, she'd swear this one was.

When she stepped into the hallway, Brendan was already there with Cedar. "Right on time," he said. "She uses regular obedience commands—'heel' to move forward, 'sit,' 'down' and 'stay.' Why don't you follow me out?"

Feather walked calmly at her side until they got outside to a grassy spot near the door.

"Okay, ah, do your thing." She felt pretty silly, walking around in the grass, trying to get the dog to "go."

"Park," he said.

"I beg your pardon?"

"That's the word you use to get her to go. I don't think she'll respond to 'do your thing.'" There was a note of amusement in his voice.

"I can't believe your dogs are trained to go to the bathroom on command. Are you serious?" She was used to pets who were let out into the backyard to sniff around until they found the perfect spot.

"Sure. You don't think I'm going to stand out here when the weather's nasty and wait until my dogs decide they've gotta go, do you?" He walked into the grass with Cedar. "Stand in one place like I am."

She did as he was doing. "I don't have to walk her?"

"Walking is good for her, but right now, no. Just tell her to park."

"Park," she repeated dubiously. "What—" But the reason for the word became instantly clear as Feather finally did her thing. Cedar did, too. Apparently the word was a magic charm. "That's it?" she asked, somewhat incredulous. "Just come out here, stand and tell her to park?"

"Yeah." He laughed. "The only other thing I'd

recommend is that you bring a bag so you can pick up if you need to."

"I didn't think of that." She eyed him. "What else do I need to know?"

"Sometimes she fools around," he said. "Sniffing and goofing off. Then I just tell her we're going in, which usually makes her remember she'd better get with the program or she's going to be crossing her legs all night."

She laughed, finding the imagery apt.

"And she absolutely hates rain and snow. If the weather's lousy, I practically have to drag her behind me. She really hates getting wet."

"Oooo-kay. So how many other things do I need to learn?"

"You have to give her a command to eat. But I can show you that in the morning."

"What about sleeping? Is she allowed on the bed? She hasn't even tried to jump on the furniture."

"She's never really been much for sleeping on the couch or the bed, unlike the big goober here," he said, indicating Cedar. "He was on the couch the first day I brought him home. But it's not off-limits unless you don't want her getting up there. I never encouraged her—that yellow hair is a whole lot more noticeable on my suits than black hair is."

She couldn't help scanning his clothing, then—and she forgot about dog hair almost instantly.

He wore only a pair of sweatpants tied low on his

torso and a disreputable Columbia Law T-shirt that was clearly from his college days. He must work out, she decided, because his chest and abs were heavily muscled as were the bulging biceps straining the arms of the shirt.

Holy cow. She'd thought he was hot before, but now…the sweats weren't tight, but as he turned to go back inside she could see that there wasn't an ounce of fat on him anywhere. His backside looked as hard and muscled as the rest of him beneath the soft fabric.

He grabbed the heavy back door and hauled it open, holding it and standing back. "Ladies first."

"Thank you," she murmured. She started forward, and after a moment Feather moved to her side and trotted obediently up the steps and inside.

As she moved up the stairs ahead of him, she reflected that it was rather pleasant to know he wasn't ogling her. She'd lost track years ago of the number of men who appeared to believe that being a celebrity, especially a model, gave them free rein to slap, pinch, fondle or otherwise handle her body. Granted, most of them were famous men who thought the world had been created solely for their pleasure, but even among the general population there were those who didn't appear to regard a model as an animate being with feelings and emotions.

"Sorry I didn't think about telling you her commands right away," Brendan said from behind her.

She tuned back in to the present. "Well, at least now I know the most important one."

He laughed. "That you do. You can walk her tomorrow if you feel like it, but if you don't have time I'll do it in the evening."

"Oh, no. If you don't mind, I'd love to walk her. But I should tell her 'heel,' not 'forward'?" She was certain that's what he said to Cedar.

"That's only for a dog in harness," he said. "She also knows a bunch more, but those are the only ones you'll need, and some of the others are only things she needed when she was working."

"All right." They were approaching their respective apartments. She fished out her key and turned. "Good night."

He smiled. "See you in the morning."

Well, she reflected as she brushed her teeth a few minutes later, she and her new neighbor had certainly gotten off on a better foot the second time around.

She hadn't mentioned him to CeCe, her sister. During their phone chat, they'd spent most of their time commiserating with each other over their father's lamentable lack of judgment.

"Why does he have to marry them?" CeCe had asked. "Why not just live with them? It's got to be less expensive when he gets tired of them if he doesn't have to pay alimony."

Lynne imagined there was some complex psychological reason for her father's need to marry each new woman, although she couldn't begin to guess at what it was. Nor did she really care. She'd accepted his failings a long time ago.

She winced as she thought of the phone call that would have to be made to her mother tomorrow. Her mother had never remarried, and each time her father found a new woman, Lynne's mother erupted in a spew of spurned anger.

Sighing, she called to Feather. The dog came happily into her room and flopped down on the rug beside her bed. Lynne spent several minutes stroking her and rubbing Feather's satiny belly.

"You're better than a man any old day," she told the dog. "If I had a dog like you, I'd never have to worry about being left alone. You'd be faithful your whole life, wouldn't you?"

She had just finished her yoga workout the following morning when the doorbell rang. Wiping her sweaty face with a towel, she opened the door to see Brendan in a sharp charcoal suit with a white shirt and soft lavender-and-charcoal-striped tie, already dressed for the day.

"Good morning," he said.

"Hi." Instinct had her cinching the arms of her black sweater around her waist before she remembered that he couldn't see her. She still felt fat in her exercise clothes. Sometimes it was hard to recall that she'd gained weight on purpose. "That's a great suit. But how do you know you have on colors that don't clash?" The man certainly was gorgeous. She'd bet that back in his college fraternity days, he'd had girls hanging all over him. Probably still did, for that matter.

"I have Braille labels in some of my clothes," he said. "And I have a fantastic dry cleaner. When I take dirty things to them, I always keep them separated in bags by outfit. So all these things I'm wearing will go in the same bag later. Then the dry cleaner reassembles the whole outfit again in a clean bag before I pick it up."

"Ah. So once you've bought something, you always keep it together."

"Right."

Feather brushed past her then and wove herself joyfully around Brendan's knees. Heedless of the suit, he knelt and petted her. "Hey, old girl. I missed you, too."

Then he rose, and she saw the bag of food he'd set beside the door. "Here's her breakfast and enough for dinner in case I'm late getting home."

"Okay." She seemed to be reduced to words of one syllable as she looked at him again. It should be criminal for a man to look so good.

"Is something wrong?" He cocked his head as if to study her, even though she knew he wasn't seeing her expression.

She expelled a rueful chuckle. "You look so nice that I'm just standing here thanking heaven that you can't see me!"

That made him laugh, too, and she felt less awkward.

"Well, now you've got me curious," he said. And before she realized it, he reached forward and unerringly settled one large hand on her shoulder.

She nearly gasped at the touch of his warm palm. His hand was so big that his thumb rested easily on the hollow at the base of her throat, and she wondered if he could feel her pulse racing.

"Ah," he said, fingering the strap of her sleeveless leotard. "Exercise clothes. What were you doing?"

"Yoga." Back to one-word answers again. Did she sound as breathless and silly as she felt?

"Sorry to interrupt. I'll let you get back to it."

"I'm finished," she said. "I do a brief workout three days a week and then go for a run, and the other three days I have a full-length routine I go through."

"That's only six." He still had his hand on her shoulder, rubbing his thumb lightly back and forth over her collarbone, and she suppressed an outrageous urge to step forward and mold her body to his. What was wrong with her?

"Um…six. Right." *Oh, Lord, help me.* "I take Sundays off, unless I feel like doing something."

"Me, too," he said. "I run every day on the treadmill and I lift three times a week."

"Can I ask another stupid question?" She was going to be rude again, but she was really curious about how he managed so well. She finally moved back just a shade, and to her mingled relief and disappointment, he let his hand drop to his side.

"There are no stupid questions, according to my old Latin teacher, only stupid answers."

"How did you know? Exactly where my shoulder was?"

He looked momentarily puzzled.

"Just now," she clarified, "when you put out your hand, you didn't fumble or grab the wrong body part, or anything. You put your hand right where you intended to."

He laughed. "How do you know? Maybe your shoulder wasn't what I was aiming for."

She shot him a dirty look, then remembered the effect would be lost. "Very funny."

"You'll never know, will you?"

"I will when you answer my question," she said firmly. This flirting was getting out of hand. He was just her neighbor, for heaven's sake. Even if he was drop-dead gorgeous and she drooled every time he threw back his head and laughed like that. She was *not* looking for a relationship. All she wanted was to settle into a nice, small town and a nice, small-town life.

"All right." He finally grew serious. "When I lost my sight, my hearing gradually started to be…I don't know, more than just the hearing that a sighted person takes for granted. Or maybe it's just that I tune in to it a lot more now. I use it—and I imagine many vision-impaired people also do—to gauge height when someone is speaking, or distance." He made a "who-knows" gesture with his hand. "I guess I've gotten pretty adept at it. It isn't something I consciously think about. I just sort of knew where your shoulder would be."

"That makes sense."

He put his hand to his wristwatch, and a moment later a voice announced the time. "I've got to go. I'll check in tonight to get my girl, if that works for you."

"That's fine." How cool was that? A talking watch. She hadn't even imagined all the things that she would have to do differently if she were blind. "Have a good day," she said.

"Thanks. You, too." He put his hand on Feather's head and fondled her soft, floppy ears with his right hand. "See you later, girl. You have a good day with Lynne."

She squatted and picked up the bag of dog food, watching as he turned away and moved purposefully down the hall. He didn't even hesitate at the stairs as he and the dog started down.

What would it be like to depend on an animal that much? She doubted she could ever come to trust a dog enough to just step forward and head down a flight of stairs that easily.

She turned and reentered her apartment as his broad shoulders disappeared. "Come on, Feather," she said. The dog still was standing where Brendan had left her, and if she were a person given to flights of fancy, she'd have said the poor thing looked sad. "Why don't we go for a walk?"

Brendan was anxious to get home that evening. It had been a long day preparing for a trial in which he was the lead prosecutor, and the rest of the week only promised to be even longer. He'd planned to take tomorrow off but he'd be lucky to manage it.

He stopped to pick up his mail, then started up the steps to the second floor. He had barely set foot in the hallway when he heard a door open.

Dog nails clicked rapidly on wood accompanied by a happy canine whine, and his heart lifted at the familiar sound. Feather hadn't sounded that happy since the day he'd brought Cedar home. While he was in class at the training school for nearly a month, she had stayed with his old school buddy with whom he worked. Feather thought John Brinkmen was the greatest guy on the planet and Brendan had no doubt she'd been spoiled rotten in his absence. Brink had brought her back the day Brendan had returned and she'd been thrilled to see him until she caught the scent of a strange dog on his clothing. It had pretty much been downhill ever since.

He caught Feather while Cedar stood patiently waiting for the next command.

"Hey, girl," he said. "Did you have a good day with Lynne?"

He raised his head. Even if he hadn't had Feather

to warn him, he'd have known *she* was there. She hadn't made a sound and she was still too far away for him to catch her scent, but he knew. "Hi," he said.

"Hi!" She sounded jazzed, excited.

"You sound happy," he said, wondering what had put that tone in her voice.

"Guess what I did today?" Her voice was jubilant.

"Won the lottery?"

She laughed. "Not even close. I bought a piano!"

"Whoa. When you decide to do something, you don't waste time, do you?"

She laughed. "It's being delivered Tuesday. And I called the college to see if I could find anyone who would give lessons. I start next week!"

"Good for you."

"I also had an interview with the preschool. They only need someone for about twenty hours a week. And the more I think about it, the more I think I'd prefer that to something full-time. This way, I can look into taking classes and maybe even start in January."

"Will you go to Gettysburg?"

"Can't. The college doesn't offer a teaching degree. But there are several schools within an hour that do. Today I looked at some schools online. Shippensburg University, Wilson College, Penn State's Mont Alto campus and Messiah College are all less than an hour away. And they all offer education degrees except for Mont Alto, but I could do the first two years there if I chose and then transfer. If I wanted to stay at Penn State I'd have to finish at the University Park campus which is more than two hours away, but I don't really want to get settled in here and then move and I don't want to drive two and a half hours one way to school each day for two years, either. So I'm going to visit Shipp, Wilson and Messiah next week."

"You have a lot of energy, don't you?" he observed in a dry tone.

She laughed. "No more than the average person, I don't think. It just seems that way because I'm starting so many new things."

He was dying to know where she'd worked before, what kind of career she'd just apparently walked away from. Maybe it was something as mundane as fast-food work, but he doubted it. Then he thought of something else.

"You do realize," he said, "that working twenty hours a week at what is probably minimum wage is not going to pay for this apartment." Let alone a new piano.

She went still. He might not have been able to see her, but he could tell from the very quality of the air that she'd practically frozen in place. Finally she cleared her throat. "I do realize that," she said quietly.

"I hope I haven't burst your bubble," he said hurriedly, regretting now that he'd said anything at all. She was an adult and her finances were none of his business. "It's none of my business. I apologize."

"It's not a problem," she said. "I should have

realized how it would look to someone who didn't know me." She hesitated. "I'm, ah…" She stopped again and chuckled nervously. "There's no polite way to say it. I'm fairly wealthy."

"That was polite," he observed. "You could have said you were loaded. Or filthy rich."

"I suppose I could have." She chuckled again, and there were far fewer nerves in her tone this time.

"Are you?"

"Am I what?"

"Filthy rich."

"Define 'filthy rich,' please."

He couldn't help smiling. "Smart-aleck. Okay. More than a million."

"Oh." Was that relief in her tone? "Yes."

She was worth over a million bucks? Was she some kind of industrial heiress or something? He couldn't figure out any polite way to ask, so he just let it go. "That's good," he said lamely.

He had fished his key from his pocket and as she spoke he unlocked his door. "Come on in," he said. "So Feather was good for you today?"

"She was delightful." She trailed after him and he heard her shut the door as he bent to remove Cedar's harness. "She just follows me from room to room. I guess she's used to always being close to someone?"

"Yeah. At work my dog lies beside my desk. She's been pretty upset at being left behind every day, even though I was trying to come home at lunch to make sure she was doing all right."

"Well, I don't mind having her hang out with me one little bit. She's more than welcome to come back anyday."

"Thanks." It was nice to know he had someone to call on in an emergency, although he couldn't possibly impose his dog on her regularly.

"Have you been over to the battlefield yet?"

"No. It's near the top of my list, though." Her voice grew warm and amused. "I think it's probably illegal to live in Gettysburg and not know anything about that battle."

"I have an auto tour on CD. You can borrow it or, if you're free tomorrow and you'd like company, I'd be happy to ride along." He was mildly amazed to hear the words come out of his mouth, particularly since he hadn't even been sure he wanted to take the day off. Had he just asked her out? He wasn't sure the casual offer qualified as a date. Still, he hadn't come anywhere near that close to dating since he'd ended his engagement a few months after his accident.

"I would enjoy that," she said. "And I'd love the company. Can we take the dogs?"

"They can come along in the car. Cedar can go anywhere we go, but now that Feather is a pet and not a working guide, I'd have to check. I'm not sure that the Park Service allows dogs on the battlefield."

"I can check," she said. "I'll get online later and

see what I can find out. If I don't get results, we can call the Park Service before we leave in the morning."

"All right. Thanks."

"Thank you. I've been wanting to look around the battlefield. This will be perfect." He could tell she was turning away as she spoke. "I'll go look it up right now."

He followed her to the door. "What time would you like to go?"

"I'm flexible. Is nine too early?"

"Nine's good."

"All right. See you then."

"Lynne." He reached out and circled her wrist before she could pull open the door. "Thank you for caring for Feather today. She means a lot to me, and it was easier to be at work knowing she wasn't alone."

She had stilled at his touch. Then, to his surprise, she turned her hand beneath his until their palms were touching, and she lightly squeezed his fingers. Her skin was warm and so soft he knew whatever job she'd held before, if any, hadn't involved manual labor. He also knew that she hadn't been any more prepared than he for the immediate sexual tension that had leaped between them. He'd felt an intense spike in his pulse when their hands touched, and from her small, stifled gasp, he suspected she'd felt the same.

Still, her tone was calm and her words were prosaic when she cleared her throat and spoke. "It was wonderful to have company," she said. "I didn't realize how solitary I am until I moved here. And I'm determined to change that." She chuckled. "Even if I have to start with a dog." Then her tone changed as she slid her hand free. "Uh-oh."

"What?"

"Feather." She sounded rather chagrined. "She's sitting by the door. I believe she thinks she's going with me again."

"Feather, come."

Silence. Great. It was going to be a repeat of dinner last night. He tried not to feel hurt. After all, from Feather's point of view, *he* was the one who had replaced *her.*

"I'd love to have her stay again," Lynne said hesitantly, "but I know you'd like her here with you."

"Yeah, but I want her to be happy…"

"She'll come around." Lynne's hand touched his shoulder lightly, rubbing a small, comforting circle. At least, he was pretty sure it was meant to be comforting. In reality, every nerve cell in his body leaped to life again at the feel of that small, warm hand.

Relationships had been on the back burner for a number of years now, but his new neighbor with the sexy voice and soft skin was getting to him in a way that was impossible to ignore.

It wasn't that he didn't *like* women, he told himself. He liked them a great deal. He'd loved one once. But after the accident in which he'd lost his eyesight, he'd been unable to believe she would want to stay with him forever. Dumb as it seemed in hindsight, he'd pushed his fiancée away, had isolated himself behind a wall of self-pity and insecurities.

It had taken him several years of counseling and healing to become comfortable with who he was now, to become convinced that a loss of sight didn't equal a loss of manhood. And by the time he'd figured it out, Kendra had moved on. He'd gone to see her one day—only to learn that she'd married. She'd answered the door of her new home and he'd felt great about the opening of the conversation, until she told him she was married.

There hadn't been much to say after that.

He'd left with the taste of defeat in his mouth, and the knowledge that he'd lost her due to his own stupidity. Since then…since then he'd had a few dates with a few very pleasant women and one hilarious disaster of a blind date. Which, in his case, took on a whole new meaning.

But of the more normal dates he'd endured, there had been no one memorable, nobody who had made his mouth water and his pulse race. It had been easy to immerse himself in his law practice, until Lynne DeVane had moved into the apartment across the hall less than a week ago.

And now?

He had no idea what she looked like, but she was memorable, all right. And it wasn't simply sexual, either. Her wry humor tickled his funny bone. She was direct and thoughtful, and she loved his dogs. She didn't even mind dog hair as a fashion accessory, which made her damn near perfect all by itself.

But there was no denying the attraction he felt. *They* felt. Because he was sure it affected her, too. The odd pauses, the pregnant silences, the electric sense of possibility that flowed between them…oh, yeah, she felt it, too.

She made his pulse race and his mouth water with just one whiff of the warm scent that clung to her skin. Her husky laugh made his whole body tingle, and the warmth of her hand made him wonder how it would feel on him.

Yes, it had been a long, long time since he'd felt this drawn to a woman, since he'd felt compelled to seek her out and explore the charged atmosphere between them.

But there was no question that he did now. And he knew exactly what he was going to do about it.

"So," he said, "after the tour of the battlefield, we'll go to the visitor center. Might as well start you out right from the very beginning."

"The beginning of my Gettysburg education?" There was laughter in her voice.

He nodded, smiling back. "The beginning of your life in Gettysburg."

"I like the way that sounds," she said with great satisfaction. "My life in Gettysburg."

Four

She would enjoy herself today.

Lynne pressed a hand to her stomach the next morning, hoping to squeeze the butterflies that were frantically fluttering around in there into submission. She checked her backpack again to be sure she hadn't forgotten anything vital, then glanced at the clock. One minute to go, if Brendan was punctual, and she'd bet her last dime that he was.

There was no need to be so nervous. It wasn't really a date. Just a neighborly excursion. He was grateful to her for her help with Feather and wanted to pay her back for dinner.

It *was* a date. At least, it certainly had sounded like

that when he'd offered his tape and his company. And then he'd planned the entire day. She suspected that as she got to know him better, she'd find a hard-core take-charge kind of guy beneath those dark suits and elegant ties that looked so good on his tall, solid frame.

Right on time, a sharp, definite knock sounded at her door. The butterflies all sprang into action.

She crossed the room and pulled the door open. "Good morning."

Feather pushed past her, and Brendan bent to fondle the dog's ears. "Good morning, and good morning. How's my girl?"

She was pretty sure he wasn't addressing her in the second sentence. "She ate breakfast and seemed content this morning. I really enjoy having her around."

"Good." His smile was broad with relief. "I worry that she's going to think I'm abandoning her."

Lord, but the man was potent. And it wasn't just that smile, although it sure didn't hurt.

She'd thought he looked good in a suit, but today, in a burgundy sweatshirt and faded denim jeans that clung to his strong thighs, he took her breath away. His shoulders looked a mile wide beneath the sweatshirt, and he'd pushed up the sleeves to reveal muscular forearms covered in silky dark hair.

How had she missed seeing just how big he was over the past few days? She was nearly six feet herself, and she barely reached his jaw, so he had to be close to six-six.

"Are your parents tall?" she blurted.

One dark eyebrow quirked upward in an expression she'd seen a number of times before, as if he wasn't quite sure how the conversation had taken such a turn. "My father is," he said. "My mother's only average height, but she has three brothers who all are over six feet." He stretched out a hand and touched her shoulder. "You're pretty tall yourself. Where did you get the height?"

"My father. My mother is only five-two." She tried to laugh. "It's not easy being the tallest girl in the class until you're in high school. I was taller than my older sister before we were even out of elementary school."

"I like tall women," he said. "My high school girlfriend was the captain of the basketball team."

"I never played basketball." She wasn't touching that first line with a ten-foot pole. "The coach was always after me to come out for the team, but I just wasn't interested. I was a dancer. For a long time I dreamed of auditioning for one of the big ballet companies. But finally I accepted the fact that no one can really use a ballerina who is taller and heavier than all the men who have to do lifts with her."

"You're not heavier than any man I know."

"Um…Brendan? Without being rude, may I ask how the heck you would know how much I weigh? I could be three hundred pounds for all you know."

"Not a chance." The hand that was touching her shoulder clasped the fragile joint, and as before, she was immediately wildly aware of how big his hand was, of how much of her skin that hand could cover if he stretched his fingers wide. "You're skinny," he pronounced, tracing his thumb over her collarbone and sliding it up to caress the line of her jaw. "In fact, I'd say you're almost too skinny."

"I am not!" If he had known her when she was modeling. And then she noticed the grin hovering around the edges of his chiseled lips. She balled her fist and lightly made contact with his shoulder. "You're teasing me."

"I might be." The grin grew broader. "Just about had you, too."

Just about had you. She was almost sure that he registered the double entendre nearly as quickly as she did. His hand stilled, and she wondered what he was thinking. *She* was having a hard time keeping her mind out of the gutter. How would it feel to have those lips on hers? To have those hands sliding over her body, pressing her against his large, hard form?

"I wish I could see your face," he said in a low, intense tone.

"Why?" She was breathless, the butterflies inside sucking all the oxygen away from her lungs.

He turned his palm to cradle the side of her face. "I'd give anything to know what your lips look like."

Her pulse stuttered and sped up even further. Before she could think of all the reasons why it was a bad idea, she reached up and took his index finger in her hand, then placed it on her lips.

Silently he traced her lips as she stood, mesmerized by the strangely intimate sensation of having him touch her face. He slid his finger around her lips, then moved down her chin, lingering for a moment in the slight cleft that she had always despised. Then he continued, tracing along her jaw and back to her ear, where he circled the fragile shell and then tugged lightly at her earlobe, exploring the three small studs he found there. She shivered, a thrill of excited nerve endings, and he left her ear to sweep back over her head. She'd done her hair up in an intricate variation of a French braid that she particularly liked because it held the straight, slippery strands of her hair in place well for long hours, and he lightly ran his hand over it, then found the bundled length of it contained in the knot at her neck. He slipped his hand beneath the coil of hair and cupped her nape. She felt herself sway toward him, but before she could complete the motion his hand was moving forward again, up to her temple, across the wide span of her smooth forehead and down the small, straight slope of her nose. He smoothed over her eyebrows and brushed her eyelashes lightly as her eyes fluttered closed—

And then his hand was gone. She opened her eyes to see him turning away.

"Thanks," he said. "I've been wondering."

"You're welcome." Her voice sounded so normal, compared to the feelings still rioting through her. Chief among them was intense disappointment. She'd wanted him to kiss her, she acknowledged to herself. She was pathetically, ridiculously infatuated with her neighbor of less than a week—and he, while he might be interested in her as a willing female, certainly didn't seem to suffer the same effects that his mere presence gave her.

"I've found that if I ask people to describe themselves, they're usually astonishing unhelpful," he said. "I get a much more accurate picture by touching."

So he did this frequently. Or, if not frequently, at least occasionally when he was getting to know someone.

It's like Braille for him, she told herself. It didn't necessarily mean anything more. It was just his way of learning a little more about me. Only fair, really, since I know what he looks like.

She felt as deflated as a hot-air balloon on the ground. "Well, now you know. Nothing out of the ordinary." She grabbed her backpack. "Are you ready to go?"

His eyebrows had done that quirky thing again at her pronouncement, but he didn't comment. "Sure."

She led the way down to her small SUV. After a moment's hesitation, she asked, "Where should we put the dogs?"

"They can go in the back together, if you put down a blanket to keep the dog hair from getting ground into your upholstery," he said. "Is there any way to keep them from being tossed forward if we were to have an accident?"

"I have a cargo net that stretches from side to side right above the back seat. Will that work?"

"Perfect," he said. "The school teaches us to put them on the floor at our feet, but most of the graduates I've met disregard that because it's too dangerous in the event of a front-end collision."

She popped the back and raised the hatch. Brendan removed Cedar's harness and patted the floor inside. "Hup up." And both dogs leaped in.

"If we were going any distance," he said, "I'd put them in kennels for safety, but since we're only going a mile or so to the battlefield and then driving five miles an hour most of the time, they should be okay."

As she walked to the driver's side, he trailed a hand along the passenger side until he reached the door, and they both slid into their seats at the same time.

"Whoa," he said as his knees practically met his nose. "Somebody a lot smaller than I am was sitting here last time, right?"

She chuckled. "My mother rode along to help me move in. There's a set of automatic buttons along the side of your seat. Press backward on the first one and your seat will move back."

"Here." He handed her a jewel case with a CD inside. "Here's the battlefield tour. Go out 116 toward Fairfield and Reynolds Avenue. Where we begin, is just a little way out of town on your right after you pass the Lutheran Seminary."

She followed his directions and easily found the correct road. Almost immediately after she turned in, the view opened up onto a sweeping vista of fields and stands of trees that sloped gently uphill at its far end. Cannons stood in occasional small formations, and along the roads she could see a number of small plaques and statues. Several miles directly ahead, a large monument with wide stone steps around it looked down over the green expanse, still lovely in early autumn. The Peace Light Memorial, he told her.

"There should be a pull-off along the road around here," he told her. "If you stop there, we can put the CD in and begin the tour. It'll tell us when and where to move."

"How many times have you done this?" she asked him.

He shrugged. "Less than a dozen, but enough to be pretty familiar with it. I've taken my folks and my sister's family, and friends who have come to visit, and my partner's parents and a few others."

"So we probably don't need the tape," she said dryly.

"Well, yeah, we do." He laughed. "I enjoy Civil War history. If you ask me to narrate, the tour might last three days instead of three hours."

They began the tour then, and talked little as they drove. Twice he asked her to describe a certain monument or scene for him. Frequently he added personal anecdotes from the diaries and stories of men who had fought at Gettysburg.

She became utterly engrossed in the saga. He showed her Cemetery Hill, where the Union forces rallied after a humiliating rout on the first day of the battle. There was the Peach Orchard, the Wheatfield, Little Round Top; names she vaguely recognized from her American history class in high school. She'd realized that walking over the grounds where so many had died would affect her. But she had never expected to be so moved by the monuments erected to honor the troops. The larger-than-life, beautifully sculpted memorial at the cemetery depicting the mortally wounded Confederate General Armistead being attended by Union Captain Henry Bingham brought her to tears as Brendan told her of Armistead's friendship with Bingham's commanding officer, Major General Winfield Hancock.

Virginia's state monument, with its clustered soldiers from different walks of life at the base and the stunning sculpture of Robert E. Lee on his horse Traveler atop the column was perhaps her favorite. "It's said to be one of the best likenesses ever done of Lee," Brendan said in a tone of near-reverence.

She smiled. "You really weren't kidding. You know a lot about this place."

"It's fascinated me since I was a kid," he said. "I was here several times before my accident, so I still remember some things."

"How does that work? Your memory, I mean." She hesitated, formulating her thoughts. "Do you still have clear memories or do they begin to fade over time?"

"I do still have memories," he said. "But as time goes by I find they get sort of blurry. Imagine it as an Impressionist painting. I have the general outline and idea, but the details are going. Handwriting was one of the first things to disintegrate."

"But how do you sign credit cards and documents?"

"I don't often use credit cards. They can be double-swiped, switched or the numbers copied and I would never know. I carry cash as much as possible, and I do a lot of ordering from catalogs and shopping at places where I've established relationships and have a monthly account. For documents, which, as you can imagine, I do have to sign quite a bit, I have a little card called a signature guide that helps me write in a given space. If you use one often enough, your muscle memory helps you keep a consistent, legible signature."

There was no anger or even resignation in his tone; he was simply uttering a fact. She marveled once again at how little his life seemed to be hampered by his lack of vision. Despite the considerable changes that had been forced on him, he had overcome most problem issues with ingenuity and grace.

Along the Emmitsburg Road, where Confederate soldiers had been urged to undertake what amounted to a suicidal effort to charge across an open field, up a hill and over Union breastworks, Brendan told her that photographs of the scene after the battle showed men lying in ordered rows where they had been cut down. "It was insane. The Union troops were massed up on the ridge ahead of you. They would wait until the Rebs got close and then they would open fire. Insane," he said again, regretfully. He told her about Pickett's futile charge, after which Pickett returned to Lee bitter and angry. "Lee told him to prepare his division for a counterattack," Brendan said, "and Pickett responded, 'General, I have no division.'"

They got out of the car a number of times to examine monuments erected by states to honor their fallen. She cried again at the sight of the Irish Brigade's tribute, a beautiful Celtic cross with an Irish wolfhound, one casualty of the battle, lying at its base.

At Devil's Den, he insisted they climb among the rocks. They left Feather in the SUV, but Lynne was surprised at how well Cedar maneuvered Brendan through the wild tumble of boulders to the small summit. "What direction am I facing?" he asked her. "It feels like north or northeast."

She had to think for a moment, squinting at the late-autumn sun. "It is. How did you know that?"

"The sun's on my face." He took her by the shoulder and turned her to face slightly to the east as he began to explain troop movements and attacks that determined the outcome of the battle. "The bottom line," he said, "is that if the Union had lost Little Round Top, the Confederates could have taken Gettysburg. In fact, given General Lee's superb leadership and the lack of any really strong, decisive Union general, it's quite likely. The whole outcome of the war might have been different. For that matter, if Lee had accepted Lincoln's request to lead the Union army, I sincerely doubt there'd even have been a war still occurring in 1863."

His face was animated, the sun lighting his blue eyes to an intense hue. She openly examined his face, wanting to touch him as he'd touched her earlier that day. Wanting more than that. She was supremely conscious of his arm, which had slid from her shoulder down her back and now curved loosely around her waist. Even through her clothing, she could feel his big hand on her.

"Lynne?" Brendan's voice was amused. "God, I'm sorry. Was I that boring?"

"No!" she said hastily, jarred from her sensual preoccupation by his assumption. "You're not boring at all. I was just trying to…to visualize it."

"And did you succeed?" He'd turned to face her, far closer than a sighted man would normally come into her personal space, and she watched as his lips formed the words.

"Sort of." She sounded silly and breathless, even to herself. "I guess we'd better get down from here and keep going."

"I guess."

Was that regret in his voice? She wondered, as she picked a careful path down through the rocks for the man and dog, if he had any idea how interested in him she was. It was silly to be so obsessed with a man. The more she was with him, the more she wanted to be with him.

They spent nearly five hours on the battlefield, and she could have spent five more. She'd anticipated missing lunch and had packed apples and ham sandwiches, which they stopped and ate while sitting on the tailgate of the SUV. As the sun began to sink toward the surrounding mountains in earnest, she turned the vehicle toward home.

"Thank you," she said when they had climbed the stairs to their floor. She stopped in the center of the hallway, midway between their doors. "That was absolutely fascinating."

"I'm glad you enjoyed it," he said. "Some people couldn't care less about the history of the area."

"I can't imagine how a person could fail to find it interesting," she said. "Next time, instead of using the tape, I'll just listen to you the whole way."

As soon as the words were out of her mouth, she wanted to sink right through the floor. He hadn't indicated in any way that he wanted to spend more time in her company.

Brendan smiled, though. "It's a deal." His watch announced the time, something she was beginning to get used to. "I'd better get going. I have dinner plans tonight."

"All right." Dinner plans. Was he subtly telling her to back off? "I need to get going, too. I—"

"Lynne." He stopped her with a finger raised to her lips. "Thanks." He captured her other hand and raised it to his lips.

Wow. If he'd been trying, he couldn't have done anything more guaranteed to melt her into a little puddle of need. She was a total sucker for a man who kissed her hand.

She didn't say anything as his warm lips firmly caressed the back of her hand; she couldn't.

Brendan stepped back and released her. "I'll see you." Then he shook his head as he grinned wryly. "Figuratively speaking."

It was only because she couldn't sleep that she heard him come in just before midnight that evening. Pure accident, she told herself, that she'd gotten a cup of tea and decided to sit in her living room and work a Japanese number puzzle until she got sleepy. And she didn't see him at all on Sunday, although she once heard him leave and later return to his apartment in the afternoon when she'd returned from church. She didn't see him Monday, either.

But Tuesday morning her telephone rang almost before she was out of bed. She stopped in the middle of her Pilates and punched the button on the receiver. "Hello?"

"Hi, Lynne, it's Brendan." She already knew that from the Caller ID on her phone. "I was wondering whether you'd be interested in having Feather anytime this week?"

"I'd love to. It's been weird and quiet around here after getting used to having a dog in the apartment."

"I know the feeling. I had to take Feather to the vet once and leave her overnight. It wasn't fun being without my partner, but it was a lot more than that. It was like being away from a member of my family. I hated it." He paused. "Well, I have to run. Bad week. I'll drop her off in a minute."

He was as good as his word. She'd barely had time to wipe her face with a towel when her doorbell rang.

"Hey," she said as she pulled open the door.

"Hey." He smiled. "Thanks a million. I tried leaving her again yesterday and she was in major mope mode last night."

"She's welcome to stay all week if you like."

To her surprise he nodded. "I would really appreciate that, if you're sure. I hate leaving her alone all day except for one brief pit stop at lunch."

"I'm sure."

"Great! Here's more dog food. Gotta run. Call me if you have any questions or problems." He'd given her his card with his contact information on it days earlier.

"We won't. Have a good…day." But she was

talking to his back as he gave Cedar a command and the two moved off toward the stairs.

Hmm. He must not be kidding about being busy.

She attended a meeting of the library's community support group Tuesday evening and promptly got shanghaied into being the treasurer, since the woman who'd been doing the job had just had an accident.

"It's temporary," the president had assured her.

But the vice president had winked. "That's what they told me ten years ago."

Feather was thrilled to see her when she returned, though she'd only been gone a shade more than an hour. She was a little surprised that Brendan didn't call to check on his dog, but she assumed it had just been one of those days.

Wednesday morning, she did her exercise routine in the house, then went for a run out Taneytown Road, which took her past the Park Service's Visitor Center and out through the southern end of the battlefield. Over the three days of combat in July, 1863, Brendan had told her, there had been clashes, conflicts and the final large-scale confrontation nearly all the way around the tiny town. Gettysburg had, at that time, been a significant crossroad, with five distinct highways leading into and through it. All but one were surrounded by or ran very close to some part of the battlefield.

Route 15 lay not far ahead of her, according to a sign. Better turn around. She had also seen a sign for the Boyd's Bear factory and an outlet mall, and she knew both of those were farther than she wanted to go on foot.

As she returned, she slowed and walked the last block to cool down. Once in her apartment, she headed for the shower and the scale. It was still habit to keep a close eye on her weight; although, these days she had the opposite problem from the one she'd struggled with while she was modeling. Now she had to be careful to eat enough to maintain the healthier weight she'd found when she'd decided to end her career.

And Brendan thought she was slender now. If he'd known her then…!

He called as she was getting lunch, but he sounded rushed, and when she assured him Feather was fine, he thanked her and the conversation ended quickly. Thursday and Friday, the same pattern repeated, and by Friday evening she was feeling the smallest sting of disappointment. He hadn't come home by seven, and she decided he must intend for her to keep Feather until Saturday. Then she heard his footsteps in the hall.

She leaped to her feet from the sofa where she'd been curled up reading a book. Feather, lying beside her, looked alert but didn't rise.

And a moment later, while she was hovering in the middle of the room, wondering what she'd say when she opened the door, she heard his door open.

And shut.

Well. It appeared that he wasn't all that anxious to see Feather, much less her.

He never said anything about seeing you.

That was true. But they'd had such a good time together last Saturday. She hadn't imagined the chemistry between them, had she?

Annoyed with herself, she went into the kitchen and spread out the financial records from the Friends of the Library. They had assured her that being the group's treasurer was no big deal, but if she had to authorize payments for a non-profit organization, she intended to thoroughly understand what she was doing.

Five

Brendan called on Saturday morning while she was stretching in preparation for another run. "Good morning," he said. "I bet you thought I had abandoned my dog."

"Not at all. You said you had a busy week." Which he had. She just hadn't expected him to drop off the face of the earth for five days.

"I'm preparing for a trial," he said. "And I've barely had time to eat."

There was a brief pause. She mentally ran through several responses, but before she could figure out what to say next, the silence had stretched uncomfortably.

"Do you have plans for today?" He didn't sound as if he thought her silence was weird.

"No," she said. "Other than going for a run this morning. I thought I might visit the Boyd's Bears factory this afternoon. Teddy bear collecting isn't really my style, but I'm beginning to think about Christmas, and my niece would love one."

"Christmas." He groaned. "Don't tell me you're one of those."

"One of those what?" She could hear the teasing tone in his voice.

"One of those organized people who spends December walking around looking smug while the rest of us try frantically to finish our shopping."

"Guilty," she said. "There's nothing I despise more than shopping in heavy crowds."

"I agree. It's tough enough maneuvering through tight aisles with a dog in harness. Trying to do it during the Christmas rush is impossible. But that's not why I called."

"I didn't think it was." A bubble of happiness at simply hearing his voice rose inside her and she laughed lightly. "Let me guess. You want your dog back?"

"No," he said. "Well, I do, but that's not why I called, either. Would you like to go out for dinner with me tonight?"

A date? Was he asked her out on a date? Completely caught off guard, she didn't answer him immediately.

"Lynne?" She thought there was a note of uncertainty in his normally self-assured tone. "I know it's probably too short notice for you—"

"I'd love to have dinner with you tonight," she said hastily. "Did you have any particular place in mind?"

"The Dobbin House. It's a local restaurant that serves nineteenth-century meals in a period atmosphere."

"I've seen the advertisements for it and thought it would be nice to try. Do you go there frequently?"

"No." His voice altered subtly, a sober note creeping in. "Not often."

What was that about? The mood had very definitely changed. "What time shall I be ready?" She didn't want him to change his mind.

"How about six-thirty?"

"Six-thirty it is. I'll look forward to it."

"So will I. I missed seeing you this week." The warmth was back in his tone, and for a moment she wondered if she'd imagined the brief change. "See you then."

She hung up the phone and stood by it for a moment, then did a quick and silly dance around her kitchen. He'd been busy. And he said he'd missed her!

The rest of the day crawled past. She washed her hair and then had a long, hot soak in the tub with her favorite bath beads late in the afternoon. She'd left herself plenty of time since her hair took a while to dry even using a dryer.

What to wear had her in a quandary. It was interesting, dressing for a date with a blind man. If he touched her, she wanted him to find the feel of the fabric attractive, sort of like she'd take extra care with makeup if he could see her. As it was, she moisturized her skin and put on the barest trace of lip gloss. She'd come here to start a regular life and the less she looked like her former self, the less chance she had of being recognized.

She should tell Brendan. Soon. He knew her well enough by now that her old life shouldn't be an issue or a novelty like it might to someone she was just meeting. But she'd only known him a week and a half, she reminded herself. It wasn't as if she were deliberately keeping a secret. There just hadn't been a good opening yet.

Finally it was six-thirty. Her doorbell rang promptly and she forced herself to walk—not skip or run—from the kitchen where she'd been standing waiting, instead of lurking just inside the door.

"Hi," she said as she pulled open the door.

"Hi." He was holding a large bouquet of roses in extraordinary shades of pink and peach and orange with some accompanying white blossoms mixed in, a sunrise in his free hand, and he extended the flowers to her. "These are for you."

"Brendan!" She was thoroughly flustered. "These are beautiful."

"Good. The woman at the flower shop described some different arrangements for me. This one sounded pretty."

"It's absolutely stunning," she assured him again. "Thank you." They were still standing in the doorway, and she stepped back. "Please come in while I get a vase and put them in water."

She hurried into the kitchen and pulled a large crackle-glass vase from a cupboard. Running the stems of the roses under water, she quickly trimmed them and arranged the lovely flowers in the vase.

Brendan had followed her into the kitchen. As she picked up the vase to carry it into the living room and place it on the narrow sofa table against one wall, he said, "What are you wearing?"

"Clothing or scent?"

"Both." He grinned. "You smell great and I just wondered what you've got on. Describe yourself for me."

"I'm not wearing any perfume. It must be whatever was in my bath beds. I think it was lily of the valley. Describe myself? Well, I'm tall."

"I already know that." His tone was dry. "And thin."

"Slender," she said severely. "My hair is long and really straight…" What else should she say?

"What color is it?"

"Blond. Very light, and my eyes are blue and my skin is quite fair when I don't have any tan. Without makeup on, I'm practically invisible."

"Hard to imagine," he murmured. "Go on."

"What else do you want to know?"

"Hair—exactly how long is it when you wear it down."

"Years ago it was almost to my waist. Right now it's just below my shoulders and I'm trying to continue to let it get longer."

"Sounds pretty."

It's a lot prettier than that curly red was. She had a horrified moment when she wondered if she'd spoken aloud, but Brendan's expression didn't change, and she breathed a sigh of relief. "I have big feet for a woman," she offered.

"Goes along with the height," he said. "I have my shoes custom-made sometimes because it's so hard to find size fourteens. Tell me about your face."

"My face? What about it?" She was mystified, and a little uncomfortable at being the focus of his attention in such a way. She was used to having her physical features analyzed but she'd never been asked to do it herself before. She also was used to her body being noticed, but it had never affected her on a personal level like this.

"What shape is it?"

"Shape? I don't know. Kind of long and thin, I guess. Oval, maybe?"

"And I already know your cheekbones are high and you have a cute little cleft in your chin."

"Which I despise."

"Why? It's sexy."

"At least I don't have to shave it. That would be a real pain."

He laughed. "Now tell me what you're wearing."

"A long skirt. And a silk shirt. I have a corduroy jacket lying on the back of the couch to wear tonight. I know it's warm for November, but it's not warm enough for one thin layer."

"Would you mind if I touched your clothing?"

"No." She took a fold of her skirt and guided it to his big hand.

"Mmm." He made an appreciative sound. "Feels like suede."

"No. I think it's brushed polyester."

Then his hand slid up the fold of skirt she'd handed him. He skimmed lightly over her hip to her back, and rubbed a small circle on her blouse. "Wow," he said. "Silky. Feels wonderful."

She didn't have a quick answer for him. Her body had tightened in anticipation at the brush of his fingers, and she was practically quivering. Good heavens, the man was potent. If he could do that with nothing more than the touch of fingertips, what would it be like if—*stop it, Lynne!* Once again, she reminded herself that she wasn't hunting a relationship. She'd had plenty of opportunities for that when she'd been modeling; not once had any man seriously appealed to her after Jeremy.

Until now.

Well, okay. So Brendan was gorgeous, too sexy to be allowed to walk around free, and more appealing to talk with than any man she could think of. It didn't mean she was going to act on her interest. Of course not.

Since it was a mild evening for November and the weather had been clear and dry all week, they decided to walk the few blocks to the Dobbin House. Brendan left Cedar at home, noting it was hard for the big dog to get out of the way in a restaurant. "His tail has been stepped on every day this week during business lunches," he explained.

He carried a white cane, and she was surprised at how well he was able to negotiate the uneven sidewalks of the old town. "If *I* couldn't see where I was going, my knees would probably be permanently skinned from falling."

His mouth quirked. "It's been known to happen. But I'm pretty careful on these sidewalks because I expect them to be uneven, so I usually do okay. Whether I'm using the dog or a cane, I find I really have to focus."

"How did you learn to use the cane? Did you have to go to some kind of school after your accident?"

"No." He shook his head. "In Pennsylvania, the Bureau of Blindness & Visual Services assigns you a mobility trainer. Unfortunately, it's done strictly by zip code and all the instructors aren't equally good. And I only got three sessions, anyway."

"Three sessions!"

"Yeah." He snorted. "I'm lucky. My family had the resources to hire a private trainer for six weeks. She was enormously helpful."

"I can't even imagine." A moment later her curiosity got the better of her when he didn't elaborate. "In what ways?"

"She taught me how much easier things could be if I learned Braille. A lot of adult-onset blind people never learn it. But now I have a special label maker and I can put special labels on my clothing so I know what matches what, which spices are which, stuff like that. I learned to use a screenreader, which translates typed messages, like e-mail and Web sites, to oral text, and I got a few assisted-living devices like my talking watch. You can't imagine all the things that are available now, although most of them are not really necessary items."

"What was your biggest challenge?"

He didn't even hesitate. "I had to adjust to using my sense of touch a lot more and to memorizing things like distances, placement of furniture. Listening to traffic patterns is another skill that takes concentration to master."

"What about people? Is it frustrating trying to figure out who's talking to you?"

"Not usually." His swinging cane detected the edge of the curb, and he stopped just as she was about to grab his arm. "Let me know when we have the light," he added. "Unless it's someone I haven't seen for years, I've found I'm pretty good at recognizing people's voices."

"I think you're amazing," she said sincerely. "I guess unless each of us is confronted with something like what you've gone through, we never know how we'd react. But I could never do what you do."

"I'm just living," he said mildly.

"Alone," she elaborated. "Independently. You support yourself, you care for two animals."

"You do what you have to do," he said. "If you'd asked me if I could handle being blind when I was a college kid, I never would have been able to imagine it. I'd have said no way."

"I suppose." But she was still doubtful. She'd meant it when she'd said he was amazing. As she got more and more used to being with him, it was hard to remember that he was blind. He was just… Brendan.

They approached the restaurant then, and she quietly directed him through the entry. After they'd hung up their coats and the hostess began to lead them to a table, he turned to her. "May I take your arm? You could guide me to our seats."

"Sure." She didn't hesitate. "Uh, right or left?"

"Left. It's called the 'sighted guide' technique. Just hold your arm close to your side and let me put my hand under your elbow. That way, you're a step ahead of me and I can tell if we're moving up or down steps or ramps, and you can keep me from banging into things."

"Okay." She moved into position and waited for him to take her left arm. He raised his right hand and sought her elbow, and his fingers brushed her rib cage and the side of her breast as he did so.

A bolt of white-hot lightning flashed and she swore she heard a clap of thunder as a surge of heat rushed through her. She closed her eyes. Had she ever been so aware of a man before?

"Lynne?"

His voice was deep and close to her ear. She turned her head to see his mouth only inches from her. What would she give to stretch up the few inches necessary to close the gap between them? She cleared her throat, determined to get her mind off Brendan and back on dinner. "I was just waiting for the hostess to show us to the table," she said lamely, starting forward.

She stopped when he was beside his chair and said, "The chair is directly to your left. The back is next to your left hand."

He put out his hand and grasped the back of the chair, easily settling himself as she moved to her own seat on the far side of the table. But when she glanced at him, he was scowling ferociously. It was the most unpleasant expression she'd seen since he'd fallen over her boxes the week before.

"What's wrong?"

His shoulders moved dismissively. "Nothing."

There was a moment of tense silence, and then he sighed. "It just really bugs me sometimes that I can't do the things I should do for a date, like seating you. Like opening doors."

"That's not important to me," she said. "Although it might be if you could see and you were just too self-absorbed to bother."

That startled a snort out of him, but she noticed his lean features relax as he chuckled. "You sound as if you're familiar with men like that."

"You can't imagine how many dates I've had that have treated me like…like an accessory," she said, thinking of several of her more boring evenings on the arm of whichever spoiled playboy was chasing her at the time.

There was a short silence. "I take it you've dated a lot of men of the 'self-absorbed' persuasion," Brendan said, a distinct query in his tone.

She was shocked to realize she'd nearly forgotten that Brendan had never seen her, that he had no idea who she had been. "Not so many," she said, trying to minimize the damage. "Maybe I just remember them vividly because they were such spectacularly bad dates."

"How about good ones?"

"Good dates? I've had some of those, too."

"Any in particular?" His voice was light but she thought she detected an intensity she couldn't quite define.

"There was one," she said, "that I thought might be a prince, but he turned out to be a toad."

"Frog." Brendan corrected her. "In the fairy tale, she kisses a frog."

"I know, but this one was definitely a toad."

"What did he do that earned him toad status?"

Oh, dear. She chose her words carefully, thinking of how she'd met Jeremy at a post-show party after a large job in Paris. "I met him when I was young and still a bit starry-eyed. He was British, and wealthy. Very wealthy, and I suppose his family had certain expectations for him. I thought he loved me, but it turned out he liked the way I adorned his arm better than he actually liked the person I was."

"How did you find out?"

Her mouth twisted and she willed herself to breathe easily. Jeremy was far in the past. "I was starting to dream about marrying him. When he realized that, he let me know in no uncertain terms that I wasn't suitable for a wife. On the other hand, he'd have been more than happy to keep me on the side after he did get married."

Brendan quietly said a word that had her eyebrows rising. "You deserve better."

"That's what I told myself." Then she gathered her courage and said, "What about you? Any—what do you call female toads? Toadettes?—in your past?"

He smiled. "No. No toadettes. If anything, I was the toad."

"How so?" She cocked her head, curious.

"I was engaged once, too." He paused a moment as if waiting for her reaction. But she carefully didn't respond, finding herself surprisingly resentful that he'd actually nearly married. How silly, when she herself had been engaged.

When she didn't speak, he went on. "It…just wasn't working out, so I ended it. She didn't want to break it off, but I insisted. So I guess I'm the toad."

"You must have had good reasons." Of that she was certain. Brendan was not the type of man to hurt someone needlessly.

"They seemed good to me at the time."

Something in his tone made her wonder…. "But now you regret it?"

"I did, later, and for a long time. But—"

The waitress approached then, and he never finished. Dinner was pleasant; the meal, interesting. Their server wore a long skirt and apron with a period blouse. The food was prepared and presented as it would have been a century ago.

As they ate, the conversation was light and easy. Brendan clearly was done with personal revelations, but she would have given a lot to know what he'd been about to say.

It wasn't as though she could ask, though. If she continued to pry, he might ask questions that would be awkward for her, as well.

And she didn't want to talk about her past. It

would be too easy to slip and say something that would make him realize that she was—or once had been—something more than simply a girl next door.

She would tell him, she promised herself. Eventually. But it was just so nice to be with someone who didn't react to her as A'Lynne, the redheaded super-model from the cover of *Sports Illustrated*.

Afterward, they walked back to their building. As they climbed the stairs, she said, "Would you like to come in for coffee?"

"Sounds great. I'd love to." Brendan followed her into the apartment and took a seat on the couch as she hurried into the kitchen. Feather immediately appropriated a place to lie down—right across the top of his feet. As Lynne worked in the kitchen, she could hear him talking in deep, gentle tones to the old dog.

Something in the quality of his voice reminded her of the way her father had talked to her when she was small. Her father. She'd avoided thinking of him during the past week. She had gotten very good at that, but Brendan's tone had pushed her mental barriers aside. Whatever else he might be, no one could ever say her father was a man who didn't love his children.

She sighed. Why did he feel compelled to marry again? She wished he'd stop tying himself legally to every woman who came into his life. Not because of any inheritance claims Lynne and her sister might have—heaven knew, Lynne had enough money squirreled away to keep her comfortable for the rest of her life, and CeCe was married to a software development engineer who owned a highly successful company. Josh was a wonderful man she'd met in college who adored her and their two children.

Hmm. That was something to think about. While neither of her parents was a stellar role model for marriage, Josh and CeCe had been married for nine years and had been together for nearly fourteen. And they were as happy as anyone she'd ever seen.

Now, where had that random thought come from? The last thing she needed to be thinking about was marriage. How silly.

She carried a small tray bearing the coffee and its accoutrements into the living room and set it down before perching on the sofa a respectable distance from Brendan.

"Did you get your piano delivered this week?" he asked after she had handed him a steaming mug.

"I did! I can hardly wait for next week!" She felt like a little kid, ready to bounce with enthusiasm. "I've been practicing scales and a few finger exercises I remember from before."

"You'll be a concert pianist in no time."

"I wish. Did you ever play an instrument?"

"Trombone, in high school. But I didn't continue in college."

"I never played anything in a band, although I always thought it would have been fun."

"It was. I went to a big high school with a very competitive band and we actually marched in the Rose Parade one year."

"Wow! I bet that was exciting."

"It was." He chuckled. "Although, I think the anticipation leading up to it was nearly as big a deal. We spent a year and a half before, raising money to get there."

"Sounds like your high school memories are good ones."

"Yours weren't?"

She shrugged. "I was taller than any boy in my class from the beginning of sixth grade on. Even by my senior year there were only a few guys taller than I was. I wasn't much of a basketball player so I didn't have anything that might have given me an identity. I loved ballet but that wasn't a school activity."

"You should have looked into modeling. Isn't height a requirement for that?"

Oh, dear. It was the perfect opening...but she wasn't ready to tell him yet. He seemed to enjoy her company now. Just her—Lynne. Once she told him who she was, she would have no way to ever know again if he was responding to her or to her image.

"I should have thought of that," she said lightly.

Not a lie, since she'd fallen into modeling purely by chance when a photographer had taken her picture at a charity event at which she'd been working for the bank where she'd gotten a job as a teller out of high school. "Add on a pretty older sister who was the captain of the cheerleading squad, and you get a girl who faded into the background most of the time."

"Hard for me to imagine," he said. "I think I would have noticed you. Even in my dopey-teenage-boy stage."

She chuckled. "You think so?"

"I know so." He set down his coffee cup. "I have to get going. I need to work tomorrow morning, clearing up the last details from the trial."

"Oh, I forgot!" She set down her cup and rose with him, following him toward the door as Feather wound around their legs. "Is it over?"

"Ended yesterday." He leaned his cane against the wall and linked his arms above his head, stretching mightily. "Thank God."

"Good outcome, I take it?"

"Of course." He grinned as he lowered his arms. "I wish I was always able to say that. This was a pretty solid case. Insurance fraud."

"Congratulations!" She punched his shoulder lightly, feeling the solid flesh beneath her balled fist. "Why didn't you say something during dinner? We could have celebrated."

"I didn't think of it during dinner," Brendan said. He reached out and settled his big hands on her shoulders, lightly rubbing his thumbs over the silky fabric of her blouse. "I was too engrossed in you."

She was too stunned to speak. Engrossed in her? Before she could summon words, he purposefully slid his arms around her, tugging her closer. "I'm going to kiss you now."

It wasn't a question, but as his face neared and his warm lips found hers, she didn't care. She put her arms around his neck, an action that allowed him to pull her more closely against him, as he took her mouth with a firm, thorough exploration that sent sizzling streams of excitement arrowing through her body.

Had she ever felt this before, this nearly irresistible urge to throw caution to the winds and give herself to this man? Had she ever felt that her flesh was going to leap right off her bones if a certain man didn't touch her?

One hand slid down her back, pressing her into the hard contours of his body, and she couldn't hold back the small sound that escaped from her throat as their bodies slid into snug proximity, fitting together as if they'd been made for that very purpose.

Brendan tore his lips from hers, stringing a feverish trail of kisses along her jaw to her ear, where he found a spot so sensitive that her knees actually buckled when his tongue caressed her there.

"Lynne." He breathed her name against her skin, raising goose bumps along the tender flesh of her arms. "I've been wanting to do this."

She smiled as her head fell back and he slid his mouth along the column of her throat. "I've been wanting you to do this."

He chuckled, then his mouth sought hers again. He kissed her strongly, deeply, repeatedly rubbing his body against hers and setting her afire so that she twisted against him and moaned.

Finally he withdrew in tiny increments, leaving her throbbing and regretful. "I've got to go," he said hoarsely, still holding her loosely against him. "Before I rush you into something you're not ready for."

She was unbelievably touched by his insight. "I'm not," she confirmed. "But you could probably change my mind," she added honestly.

He groaned. Dipping his head, he pressed one last, hard kiss against her mouth. "Do you have to make it harder?"

The moment he said it, silence fell between them. A heartbeat passed, and then he ruefully said, "Poor choice of vocabulary," as he set her away from him.

She laughed, delighted with his frankness. "We'll pursue that another time."

"God, I hope so." His words were fervent and he smiled as he picked up his cane and his hand sought the door handle. "I'll call you tomorrow."

* * *

Brendan paused inside his own apartment. Cedar was kenneled in the kitchen, and the metal rattled as the dog anticipated his release. "I'm coming, buddy."

He negotiated easily through his apartment and released Cedar from the kennel, stroking the broad head as the dog pressed himself joyously against Brendan. "I love you, too, buddy," he said aloud. "But I sure wish there was someone other than you touching me right now."

His breath was still fast and shallow from the moments with Lynne as he clipped on a leash and led Cedar down to the park at the rear of the building. He hadn't been looking for a relationship. In fact, it had been so long since he'd even been interested in learning more about a woman that he had been starting to think that perhaps his lack of interest was related to the fact that he could no longer see them.

Now he knew that couldn't have been more wrong. He just hadn't met the right woman.

He entered his apartment again, still aroused by the mere thought of Lynne's slender curves and sweet mouth. As he removed his pants and his hand brushed against his own hard flesh, he groaned, wishing relief could be that easy. But he wasn't going to be satisfied with anything less than his pretty neighbor stretched out beneath him in his bed, her long, slender legs wrapped around his hips and her body arching against him as he pleasured her.

That would, indeed, be satisfying.

Dropping his hand, he padded naked across the hall to the bathroom. He'd never been a fan of cold showers but tonight might just be the exception to the rule.

Six

There was a message from Brendan on her answering machine when she got home from church the next day. Did she want to go hiking in the Michaux State Forest?

Yes! Her heart leaped at the sound of Brendan's voice, and her fingers trembled as she called him back.

When he answered, he sounded strangely diffident as he repeated the invitation. "There's only one catch," he said.

"What's that?"

"You have to drive."

"Oh, I don't mind driving," she said quickly. If driving meant she got to spend the afternoon alone with him, she'd drive across the country.

The hike was pleasant, as the weather was still mild. The path was a wide, well-traveled one that Brendan and Cedar had no trouble covering. The first half, however, was nearly all straight uphill, and by the time they reached a plateau that looked out over a nearby ridge, she was almost panting.

Brendan, she noticed, didn't even look as if he'd broken a sweat.

"No fair," she said. "How can you make this look so easy?"

His smile flashed. He was wearing jeans today that faithfully hugged the strong contours of his thighs and—though she tried not to stare—closely molded to the bulge in the front of his jeans. His light-green sweatshirt emphasized his tanned skin and dark hair and she knew that her breathlessness wasn't all due to the climb.

"Faithful exercise," he said.

"Hey! I exercise faithfully!"

"Maybe I'm just naturally in better shape than you."

She snorted, showing him her opinion of that, and he laughed. Then he turned and gestured to the view before them. "Tell me what you see."

"How do you *do* that?" she demanded, stepping to his side.

"Do what?"

"How do you know which way is the view?"

"Well, much as I'd like to claim I can sense it," he said, "this one is a no-brainer. We came up the hill, and I turned to talk to you. But Cedar is still standing in the same position he was when we reached the top. And I already knew the open view was straight ahead at the top of the trail since I've been here before."

He reached for her hand and a warm glow spread through her as he laced her fingers between his. "So tell me what you see."

She cleared her throat, trying to think past the surge of her pulse and haze of awareness clouding her brain.

"Ah…the leaves are mostly off the trees now, and the tree bark makes the mountain look sort of silvery. It's a pretty day and the sky is very, very blue. Down in the valley between the two mountains is a river, and since we had a wet summer, the water level is still high and there are splashes of white where a few small waterfalls have formed."

"Very nice images. I had been here with my college roommate before the accident. I can still picture it in my head, but it's nice to hear your description. It really brings it back."

"Did your roommate live in this area?"

"He still does. That's who I work for."

"So that's what drew you to Gettysburg."

"That's what drew me to Gettysburg," he confirmed. He picked up Cedar's harness handle. "We probably should start down again. I have dinner plans this evening—a working dinner, actually—and I have to prepare."

As they hiked back down the hill, she found herself amazingly content. He hadn't invited her to do anything that evening—but he'd told her the circumstances of his outing rather than leave her to wonder whether or not he had another date.

She volunteered for the first time at a local soup kitchen the next day. Her fellow volunteers were mostly retirees who had known each other for years, but they were so warm and welcoming she felt as if she'd been there forever by the time the last dish had been dried and put away. When they learned she was free and interested in volunteering some more, they promptly shanghaied her to help deliver meals to people who were homebound every day for the rest of the week.

She suspected Brendan was having another busy week because she didn't hear from him for two days, and she was glad she was busy. She hadn't heard anything more about the preschool application she'd sent in. On Monday she attended an executive committee meeting of her library group, where she learned more than she'd ever expected to know about the cost of transferring selected historical texts onto CDs. That evening she got out a brush Brendan had sent along with Feather's food and gave her a thorough brushing out in the backyard of the building. She figured if she saved all the hair she collected, in about a year she'd have enough to knit a sweater.

She had her first piano lesson on Tuesday and was working on some new finger exercises that evening when the doorbell rang. She nearly broke her ankle rushing to the door because Feather darted in front of her determined to beat her to it. But it was worth it when she opened it to see Brendan on the other side, looking ridiculously hot and handsome in a black suit with a white shirt and conservative burgundy tie.

"Hi," she said.

"Hey. Did I hear music?"

She nodded, then remembered to speak. "Yes. I had my first piano lesson this afternoon. Would you like to come in?"

He shook his head. "I have to go back to the office this evening. But I wondered if you'd like to go to a community concert with me tomorrow evening. The featured performers are a jazz quartet that's pretty well-known."

"That sounds nice. I'd love to." *He just asked me on another date!*

"I'll knock on your door about seven," he said. "It starts at seven-thirty, so we'll have plenty of time to walk over. It's at the high school."

He was as good as his word the following evening, and they strolled over to the school for an evening of jazz. Cedar lay down at Brendan's feet the entire time, seemingly asleep. At intermission she said, "I can't believe the music doesn't bother him."

"His puppy raisers used to take him to their kids' band concerts. He's a music buff from way back."

She laughed. "A cultured dog."

After the concert they walked home again, and to her utter pleasure, Brendan put Cedar on a stay and then kissed her at her door, leisurely exploring her mouth and urging her closer to his hard body until she had to tear her mouth away and draw a breath.

He leaned his forehead against hers. "You are a potent package, lady."

"Thank you," she said, "I think."

"I'm pretty tied up tomorrow and Friday," he said, "but if you'd like to get together on Saturday, I'm game."

"I need to do some Christmas shopping at the outlets," she said. "Not fun but necessary. You can come along if you like."

"That would be great. You can help me pick out gifts for my mom and my sister."

"But I don't even know them," she protested. "How will I know what they like?"

"I know what I want and their sizes," he said. "You can be my style and color consultant."

"I can give that a shot."

Tuesday evening, Lynne opened her door as he was fitting his key into the lock and invited him for dinner, but he had to pass because he was going back to the office for a seven-o'clock meeting. "Are you going away for Thanksgiving?" he asked.

"Yes. My sister is having Mom and me for the meal." She hesitated. "Would you consider letting me take Feather along? I promise I won't let my niece and nephew harrass her."

"That would be fine." He'd been worrying about how both dogs would do at his parents' house. His dad was driving down to get him tomorrow evening and it had been on his mind.

"That's great!" she said. "I'll only be gone overnight, because I'm not leaving until Thursday morning."

"No problem." He stepped closer, snagging her by the waist and tugging gently. "Come here and kiss me goodbye."

"Goodbye." As his lips met hers, he could feel her smiling.

On Wednesday morning, he had to go down to the Franklin County courthouse in Chambersburg, nearly an hour's drive away. It didn't take as long as it might have, because he caught a ride with a local deputy who was driving down for a trial, and the guy drove as if he was an entry in the Indy 500. Even without sight, Brendan could tell they were moving a lot faster than the speed limit.

The deputy had the radio tuned to a country station and proceeded to sing along at top volume. Off-key. Brendan wouldn't have been surprised if Cedar, kenneled in the back of the big SUV beside the deputy's patrol dog, had started to howl.

As they passed the turnoff for the Michaux State

Forest, his thoughts immediately turned from the case he should be reviewing to the past weekend. To Lynne.

The shopping trip on Saturday had gone well, in his estimation. He'd hated shopping even when he'd been sighted. Now it was torture. But with Lynne, he'd barely noticed the annoyances. She'd matter-of-factly given him directions and if she'd minded the extra time he was sure the trip had taken, it never showed.

In fact, she took his lack of sight in stride better than some people he'd known for years. Like his own mother, who hovered anxiously every time he went home, asking him frequently how she could help him. For a long time it had annoyed him. Now he just let it roll off, knowing his sister was sitting on the other side of the room smirking. His sister, Jeanne, married with two young children, was usually the object of their mother's almost compulsive need to help, so she enjoyed the respite whenever he came home.

Lynne, on the other hand, never assumed he couldn't do something. If he needed help, she responded in a low-key way. She asked good questions when she didn't understand something. He knew Jeanne would like her.

He wanted to take her home to meet his family, maybe at Christmas, although he hadn't told her yet. They'd only known each other for three weeks.

Only three weeks…and in those three weeks, he had quickly recognized that nothing in the life he had led so far had prepared him for the emotions he was beginning to feel in connection with the tall, sweet-tempered woman across the hall.

He was walking through a hallway on the second floor when he heard a woman's voice say, "Brendan?"

He stopped, instantly swept into the past, but unsure if he was imagining things. "Hello?"

"Brendan." The voice drew closer, and he heard a woman's light steps tapping across the floor. "It's Kendra. I thought it was you and then I saw your dog and that clinched it. How are you? What are you doing here?"

A hand touched his forearm, and he automatically raised his own and clasped it. "I'm good. Just down here for a case. How about you?"

"I haven't seen you in so long." She fell silent, and an awkward moment passed as she clearly remembered the last time she'd seen him. "I'm here to get my passport renewed. Joe and I are hoping to travel to Ireland in the summer to visit my grandmother. Remember her?"

He did, indeed. A fiery little Irish lady, Kendra's grandmother had come over for Christmas once while they were in school. "I do. Is she doing well?"

"Oh, yes. We're going because…well, I'm pregnant, due in February, and we want her to see the baby. She's getting too old to want to fly anymore."

"Congratulations." He smiled, meaning it. "You're going to be busy in the new year."

"Yes. I can't wait. I'm sort of hoping for a girl, but

I know once I hold this baby in my arms I'm not going to care one little bit." Her voice bubbled with enthusiasm, but Brendan recognized nerves beneath the bouncy tone.

"I really am happy for you, Kendra," he said quietly. "I wish things could have worked out differently. I was a jerk and I'm sorry for that."

"You weren't a jerk." Her voice was low and gentle. "You were a man dealing with a life-altering event in the best way you knew how." Her voice changed, becoming teasing. "It was the wrong way, obviously, since you weren't smart enough to keep me."

"My loss. Joe's a lucky guy." He smiled. They'd been close once and although their lives had taken paths far different from the one they'd once expected to tread together, he had fond memories of their youthful years together.

"Is this a new dog? Last time I saw you, you had a golden retriever."

"Feather. I retired her not long ago. This is Cedar and he's working out very well." He went on to tell her a little more about Cedar, and after a few more moments of small talk, she stretched up and kissed his cheek and they parted ways.

He got called into court shortly after that and didn't really have time to think about the encounter until the trip home, with Deputy Depree singing "These Boots Were Made for Walkin'" beside him.

When he got home, his father would probably be

waiting, and he and Cedar would be off to his parents' home for a few days. He wished Lynne could go with him.

And he suddenly realized just how much he'd been thinking of her over the past few days. It had been nice to run into Kendra, but there was no pain like the last time, when he'd gone to her house to tell her he wanted her back—and found out she'd gotten married.

No, this time he was genuinely happy for her. He had Lynne now, and the old sting was gone. In fact, there was little comparison between his boyish feelings for Kendra and what he was beginning to feel for Lynne. Holy hell. Was he actually considering the implications of the "M" word?

Marriage. In retrospect, he'd taken Kendra's love as his due. Everyone grew up, fell in love and got married. At least, that had been his distinctly shallow view of the world back then.

He had cared for Kendra. But their relationship had been based largely on sheer sex appeal, like any healthy young animal. With Lynne, there was more. They shared some interests, enjoyed each other's differences. She'd been pleased when he'd won his last case; he'd been delighted that she'd taken up piano again. He tried to make her laugh just for the pleasure of hearing the musical sound, and he appreciated that she didn't seem to view his blindness as something that made him less or different.

He hadn't made love to her—yet—but he was

pretty sure that when he did, the explosion would be able to be seen in Taiwan. So, yeah, the physical attraction was definitely part of it. He could hardly wait to take her to bed, because it would be one more link between them, as well as being the best damn thing that had ever happened to him in his entire life.

Since he'd chosen to walk away from Kendra, marriage had always been a someday-down-the-road occurrence, and he'd been in no hurry to pursue it. But now…now the daydream had a face and a voice. He could picture living with Lynne, sharing the little moments that made up a lifetime together.

And kids. A wild sense of anticipation rushed through him. He hadn't pressured her so far but that was about to change. Both because he wanted to tie her to him so thoroughly she'd never even think of wanting to get away, and because his patience was wearing thin.

He wanted to know everything there was to know about her, but she was amazingly reticent for a woman, and unless he asked directly she rarely volunteered information about herself. He was keenly aware that she still held a deeply private part of herself away from him—away from everyone.

He fully intended to stay with her, to keep her with him until they were parked side by side in rockers on the front porch of a nursing home. So she was just going to have to get past that little tendency to hold part of herself back.

As he'd anticipated, his father was waiting when he returned. And Lynne wasn't home, much to his intense disappointment. He hadn't realized how much he'd counted on introducing her to his father. Feather barked from inside and he called to her through the door before he left, feeling vaguely guilty, though he knew Lynne already loved her and would take care of her as well as he could have done.

But it was with some reluctance that he gave Cedar the "Forward" command and started out of the apartment building behind his father.

Thanksgiving at CeCe's house had been a whirl-wind of parades, pumpkin pies and pesky children who begged her to play games incessantly. "Just one more, Aunt Lynnie? Please?"

How was she supposed to resist that? Her niece was great with Feather, especially once she explained that Feather was an older lady and probably wouldn't want to chase their balls or run around the yard much.

All in all, it had been an extremely pleasant visit. Neither she nor her sister had mentioned anything to her mother about her father's newest marriage, so the holiday had been fairly tranquil. If they could just make it through Christmas, they could tell her—and then she'd have a good while to rant and rave. Hopefully, she would have vented the worst of her outrage before another big family event.

* * *

She knocked on Brendan's door after she brought her luggage up from the car Friday afternoon, but there was no answer. Oh, right. He was probably working.

But she didn't hear his footsteps at all Friday evening or Saturday. He must have gone away for the holiday weekend. Intense disappointment stung her and she caught herself holding back tears several times.

Once again it appeared she had presumed too much.

She remembered vividly the conversation they'd had about Thanksgiving. She'd told him her plans—but she hadn't heard his. In hindsight, it was a pretty clear sign that he wasn't ready for intimacy on a deeper level.

And that was okay with her, because neither was she, she assured herself vigorously. She was just disappointed because they'd been spending so much time together.

She'd talked to her father last night. Well, mostly she'd listened while he babbled on and on about his new bride. He thought he was in love. And, truly, he sounded like it. But she knew it wouldn't last. Which made her wonder how in the world she could ever trust her own feelings.

Right now she felt strongly attracted to Brendan. If she wanted, she could daydream about a house with a white picket fence, two kids and a minivan. The dog was a given. But…

I don't own him, she reminded herself. Nor do I want to.

Right. Fibber.

She sighed. She couldn't deny that she found Brendan enormously attractive—

Bang! Bang! Bang! "I know you're in there."

Brief silence.

Then the overly enthusiastic knocking—which was, she realized, what the banging sound was— began again. "Open up, Brendan." The voice was male, deep and colored with frustration. "I just found out about Kendra's pregnancy, and I know she told you. Are you okay?"

Pregnancy? Kendra who? Why would Brendan be upset about it? A fist clutched her stomach into a painful knot.

Oh, stop it! There could be a dozen explanations.

Feather chose that exact moment to begin to bark.

"Feather!" Lynne hissed the name, trying not to let the visitor know anyone was there. But the dog was beyond hearing. She ran to the door and, in the first such display Lynne had seen her make, began to paw at the kick plate and whine, occasionally stopping switching to high-pitched, happy barks.

The banging on Brendan's door stopped. Then she jumped a foot in the air as the person in the hallway transferred his fist to her door.

"Feather? Is that you, Feather? Hey, Brendan, if you're in there, open the damn door!"

She stood. If the dog liked him, the stranger

couldn't be dangerous. Unlocking the dead bolt, she pulled open her door.

The moment the door opened, Feather shoved her way through it and made straight for the man on the other side. He was about as tall as she was, blond, deeply tanned and rugged looking, with thick eyebrows over piercing, blue eyes. If they weren't in Gettysburg, she'd swear he had just walked off a beach with his surfboard.

"Hey!" he said by way of greeting. He knelt, and Feather rolled over onto her back so that he could vigorously rub her belly. "How's my best girl?" he crooned. "My Heather-Feather. Have you missed me?"

He glanced up at Lynne and grinned, apparently not caring a bit that she'd just heard him speaking baby talk to a dog. "Sorry. Feather and I are special pals."

"I see that." She extended her right hand. "I'm Lynne DeVane."

He rose and clasped her hand in his for a moment, shaking it firmly. "I'm John Brinkmen, Brink to my friends. Brendan and I work together." He openly assessed her from head to toe. "You must be new. Brendan's neighbor, the one I remember who lived here, was small and white-haired, and he, uh—" he grinned "—he sure didn't look like you."

She nodded, unsure what to say, but Brendan's friend barely paused for breath. "Do you know where he is?"

She shook her head. "He was gone when I got back here Friday and I haven't spoken to him."

Brink's easy smile faded a bit. "Then why do you have his dog?"

"Feather's been staying with me most of the time since I moved in." And why was she explaining herself to this man whose eyes were growing increasingly suspicious? "She hasn't been happy about sharing Brendan with Cedar, and she seems to prefer living over here." She knelt and called the dog, and Feather came to sit obediently at her side. "I love having her."

Brink's expression relaxed somewhat as the dog's relaxed manner registered with him. "I see. He told me he'd been having some problems integrating Cedar into the equation. But I wonder why he never mentioned you."

She shrugged. "There's nothing really to mention. He's a good neighbor." *And my nose is probably growing. Nothing to mention, my foot.*

One blond eyebrow rose. "I see."

She sincerely hoped not. There was nothing worse than looking like a lovesick fool, especially in front of the object of your affection's closest friends. "I'd be happy to give Brendan a message when he returns."

"I'd appreciate it if you'd tell him I stopped by." Brink waved a mobile phone in the air. "I've left him voice mails and texts all day but he hasn't answered." Then he paused and looked searchingly at her. "Have we met? You look awfully familiar."

An alarm bell sounded. "No." She spread her hands. "A lot of people say that. I must just have one of those faces."

Brink was still examining her. "I guess." Then he smiled and held out his hand again. "Good to meet you, New Neighbor Lynne. Thanks for passing on my message."

"You're welcome. Nice to meet you, too."

But as she took the dog back into her apartment, her thoughts were consumed by what she'd heard. Who was the pregnant Kendra? And why wouldn't Brendan be okay with it? There was one obvious answer: a man who didn't want to be a father wouldn't be pleased at learning he was about to become one.

Seven

An hour later Lynne was about to head for bed when Feather started to bark and she heard Brendan's footsteps on the stairs. She would let him get settled in, she decided, stifling the urge to run to the door. She would have plenty of time Monday evening to pass on his friend's message.

He was speaking to someone, and she heard a second set of footsteps, both of which stopped outside his door. Deep, masculine voices rumbled for a few moments, and soon one set of footsteps moved off toward the stairs at the end of the hall.

Then, instead of heading into his own apartment, Brendan's footsteps crossed to her door. Feather went wild, prancing and leaping, although she didn't bark as she had earlier.

Sighing, she went to the door. Might as well get it over with. Part of her was anxious to see him. Too anxious. The other part was fighting feelings of hurt and insignificance.

"Hello," she said. "Welcome home."

"Thanks. I missed you." He reached for her, but she stepped back and he only caught her hand. After a moment's awkward silence, he asked, "Did you have a good holiday weekend?" He released her hand and bent to fondle Feather's ears.

"Yes, very nice. You?"

"Pleasant. I went to visit my family. But it's a relief to be coming home to my own place again. And I think Cedar had enough of being stalked by my mother's cat."

She couldn't help chuckling at the image of the big black dog backing away from a cat. Then she remembered she was striving for reserved and calm, and she composed her features.

"How did Feather do on your trip?"

She gave him a quick briefing and then took a breath. "A friend of yours came by today."

"Who?" He didn't sound more than idly interested.

"John Brinkmen."

"Oh, Brink. I don't claim him as a friend." Brendan grinned, and she sensed that he was determined to keep the conversation easy and pleasant. "Although the line loses some of its punch without him around to hear it."

"I let Feather go visit with him. She was having conniption fits in here once she heard his voice."

"I bet. When I got my first dog, some more-experienced guide dog users warned me that almost every dog has some person they react to, some person who makes them lose all common sense and training and act like a total idiot. Brink is Feather's downfall."

"It was rather obvious."

"I finally convinced them both that she had to behave and act like a guide at the office. But at home…" He shook his head in amused dismay.

"He mentioned something about a Kendra, too. He was concerned about you." She tried hard to keep her voice expressionless.

Brendan went still. "Exactly what did he say?"

"Just that he knew you'd found out she was pregnant and he was worried about you. You should probably call him."

Brendan exhaled. "Or maybe I'll just go over there and strangle him."

"What?" She was startled out of the careful calm she'd been cultivating.

He raised a hand and rubbed the back of his neck. "I owe you an explanation."

"You don't have to explain anything to me, Brendan. It's not like we—"

"Lynne." His voice sliced through her babbling. "Do not finish that sentence."

She didn't know what to say in response to that, so she said nothing.

"Give me ten minutes to park the dog and take all my stuff inside. My dad and I set all my suitcases in the hallway."

"All right." She would have offered to help but she sensed he needed the time.

"I'm going to stick my head out the door and yell, and when I do, you're coming over." It wasn't a question.

"All right," she said again. There were times when it just wasn't worth arguing. For some reason Brendan had taken exception to something she'd said and she was fairly sure she was going to find out exactly what it was in about ten minutes.

He yelled across the hall in exactly nine minutes. When she entered his apartment, there was only one light burning, and the room was dim.

"Sit down," he said. "I poured us some wine." He indicated two glasses on the coffee table before the couch.

Silently she took the seat he indicated and shifted to face him as he sat beside her.

Once seated, though, he didn't speak immediately. Instead, he took her hand and sat, rubbing his thumb across the backs of her much-smaller fingers. Finally he said, "I do owe you an explanation. It just never occurred to me that it was important."

He picked up his wine with his free hand and took

a sip. "I mentioned before that I had a steady girl-friend in college. Her name was Kendra."

Lynne's heart sank. So he'd known her for a long, long time.

"We got engaged at Christmas of our senior year. In February I had the accident." He didn't have to elaborate; she knew what he meant. "I also told you I was the one who called off the wedding a few months later."

She managed a noncommittal "Mm-hmm?" to encourage him to continue.

"Kendra got married a couple of years ago. She lives in Chambersburg. I was at the Franklin County Courthouse the other day and I ran into her." He shrugged. "In all honesty, I never would have known she was there if she hadn't said something. It was...nice...to talk to her. She's pregnant and expecting her first child soon."

She was so relieved she couldn't speak if she wanted to. It wasn't his baby! Not that she'd really thought it was...she just hadn't known *what* to think.

"Anyway," he went on, "my obnoxious friend and partner apparently found out, and I guess he thought the news would drive me to suicide. Hence the idiotic trip over here."

She found her voice. "He was just concerned. It was nice of him."

"Huh." In one short syllable, Brendan made it clear what he thought of Brink's concern.

Then he shifted, drawing her closer and sliding his arm around her. "I apologize for not staying in touch over the past few days. I went to visit my family for Thanksgiving. I intended to come back on Friday but my mother talked me into staying through the weekend. I should have called—but I realized I only have your number at my office."

"It's all right," she said. "You don't owe me—"

"Dammit, Lynne!" His voice was explosive, and she jumped. "Why are you constantly trying to downplay what's happening between us?"

"I'm not," she protested. "But I don't have any claim—"

"Maybe I want you to," he said in a low, ferocious tone that caught her totally by surprise. And before she knew what was happening, he jerked her toward him and set his mouth on hers.

He kissed her with a stunning, single-minded intensity that rendered her too shocked to move for a moment. His tongue boldly sought hers, his lips dominated and devastated her pitiful defenses. Finally she put her hands up to his shoulders—to push him away?—but he only reached up with one hand and dragged her arm up behind his head. At the same time he pushed her backward onto the couch, using the broad planes of his chest to lay her down as he slid one hand unerringly up beneath the thin sweater she wore. There was nothing tentative about his touch as he pushed her lacy bra aside and filled his palm with her breast.

And still he didn't speak as he rolled and rubbed her sensitive nipple, fanning a wildfire of desire deep inside her.

She couldn't speak, couldn't move, couldn't think; she could only lie there and *feel*. Brendan slid one muscled knee between her legs, dragging the fabric of her skirt aside so that she felt a rush of cooler air over her lower limbs. He was kissing her again, sapping her will and dragging her under a crashing wave of wanting.

"Brendan." It was the gasp of a drowning woman.

"Lynne. I want you," he said, his voice deep and hoarse. "I've been going crazy wondering if you've thought of me as much as I've thought of you."

The words melted any resistance she might have offered. "I did. I have." But he already had his mouth on hers again, kissing her almost frantically. He slid his lips along the line of her jaw and she felt the hot blast of his breath on her sensitive earlobe a moment before he sucked it into his mouth and swirled his tongue around it. An unexpected bolt of white-hot desire flashed through her, and she sucked in a breath as her body arched against him.

"Wait!" she gasped, not entirely sure what she even meant.

But he only shook his head as his mouth traveled down her throat and sought her breast, beginning to suckle her, right through the fabric of her shirt and bra. "Can't."

A distant part of her felt him reach down, his big hand moving purposefully between them, and then suddenly, shockingly, his hard body was there, the steely length of him pushing at the moist, tender entrance to her body as he pulled aside her thong.

Instinctively she tried to close her legs but he controlled her easily, one big hand pulling her thigh up around his waist. He pushed, pushed, and suddenly her body gave way and he slid into her, pressing steadily forward as her body accepted his hard possession. She felt a slight pinch of discomfort and then her slick readiness eased his path. As he surged heavily into her, she groaned, sure she could take no more.

Just as steadily he withdrew and thrust forward again. She clung to him, her body overwhelmed by his hard aggression, the rough delight of his urgency tightening the need coiling in her belly as he repeated his actions. She lifted her legs higher around his waist, her heels pulling him to her, and the shift in position exposed her to his thrusts in an even more intimate way that caught her off guard as waves of heated pleasure rolled through her in rhythm with his movements.

He pounded into her faster and faster, his slick muscles hot beneath her hands as she pulled his shirt out of the way and ran her hands up his back.

She couldn't think, couldn't breath, couldn't do anything but let the spiraling excitement build. Then she screamed, the sound muffled against his shoulder, as he slid one hand between them and pressed a finger firmly against her. Her back arched and she convulsed beneath him as rhythmic waves of release shuddered through her. Above her, she dimly heard him make a deep sound of pleasure as her body squeezed and clenched his swollen shaft. And then his motions disintegrated into frantic intensity until he froze above her, his arms shaking as he held himself still, pouring himself into her in long, liquid jets of heat until he collapsed onto her in boneless satisfaction, turning his face into her neck and pressing his lips against her.

His back heaved beneath her hands as he gasped for breath. His body was heavy, but when he would have moved she made an incoherent sound of denial and pulled him closer.

He gave a low laugh as he nuzzled her neck and then sought her lips. "Can a person die of pleasure?"

She smiled. "I never thought so before tonight."

He did move then, though she protested, sliding out of her and rolling to one side. Before she had time to feel bereft, he turned and pulled her into his arms. Her body felt heavy and lethargic, and her last thought before her eyes closed was that she would be happy for the rest of her life if she never had to move from this spot again.

A while later—she had no idea how much time had passed—Brendan stirred, his muscled chest moving beneath her head. A finger slipped under her chin and lifted her face to his, and she responded wholeheartedly as he kissed her again and again.

Finally he pulled his head back a fraction. "What have you been thinking for the past couple of hours?" he whispered against her mouth.

"I thought you might be in love with someone else," she blurted. The moment the words hit the air she wanted to crawl into a hole and never come out. She couldn't believe she'd said that aloud.

Brendan had gone perfectly still. She couldn't blame him. Sex, especially to men, didn't necessarily have anything to do with love.

Then he shifted, pinning her beneath him again. "And that bothered you?"

She hesitated, then whispered, "Yes." She'd already blundered; why try to fix it now?

"That's good," he said with great satisfaction, and his hands were tender as they traced the bones of her face. "Because I'm falling in love with you and I'd hate to think I was the only one affected."

"Oh, Brendan…" Her throat closed up and she couldn't speak. She was too happy. It was scary to be this happy, to know that another person could hold your world on the tip of one finger.

He kissed her again, and against her belly she felt his body stirring to life. She reached down between them, and he groaned with pleasure as her seeking fingers circled him, tracing the hard flesh she found from the tip to the crisp thatch of curls at its base.

She forgot any thought of talking then as he lay back and reached for her, drawing her up to straddle his hips. An involuntary shiver of excitement rushed through her at the feel of him solidly nestled against her soft, wet flesh, and he gave a low chuckle of lazy pleasure. "We can talk later. Right now I can think of better things to do."

Brendan was barely through the door of his office the next morning when Brink rushed in behind him. "So just how serious are you about your gorgeous blond neighbor?"

"Who says there's anything serious going on?" He waited a beat, but he couldn't stand the suspense. "Gorgeous, huh? What does she look like?"

"Hot," Brink said promptly. "Very, very hot. Tall, legs long enough—"

"Her face," Brendan said sharply. "Just her face."

"She's pretty," Brink said simply. "She wasn't wearing makeup the day I saw her, and I don't think I'd have picked her out of a crowd right away, but it wouldn't have taken long once I'd gotten a good look at her face. Great cheekbones, full lips, dimples. That damnably sexy dimple in her chin. Nice teeth. Big blue come-hither eyes—"

"Okay. You can stop there."

Brink laughed. "Uh-oh. Jealousy gene kicking in?"

"No need. She's mine."

"Are you kidding me?" Brink sounded astonished.

"Not one little bit. Hands off, buddy boy."

"Damn." Brink sounded aggrieved. "There's no justice in the world. You can't even see her and you still get the hottest woman in this town. You could have found a sweet girl, a girl with a wonderful personality, a girl with wit and charm. It wouldn't have mattered if she was uglier than a mud fence, but no, you have to take one of the pretty ones."

Brendan nodded with satisfaction, laughing hard. From the very day of his accident, Brink had been irreverent and amusing, refusing to dance around the topic of Brendan's blindness. "A mud fence, huh? Thanks so much for thinking of me."

"No problem. What are friends for? So are you going to bring her to the Christmas party?"

"The thought had crossed my mind. Have you managed to snag a date yet?"

"Amanda from the accounting firm across the street."

"The one you've been taking to lunch? The one you said looked like a Meg Ryan who is quiet and mysterious?"

"The very one."

"Way to go."

"Yeah. We're going to have the greatest dates in the room." Brendan heard the sound of his friend's footsteps heading for the door. Then Brink turned around again. "So, you never answered me…how serious are you about her?"

He didn't hesitate. "Very."

"Like rings and vows serious?"

Brendan nodded. "Yeah. But we haven't known each other very long. I don't want to rush her."

"I don't know, bro," said Brink before he headed to his own office. "That is one incredibly gorgeous girl. You'd better not wait too long."

Lynne's cell phone rang that afternoon as she was walking home from a new-member meeting at the church she'd begun attending. She had Feather with her since the pastor had told her it would be fine to bring the dog along. Happiness rose as she glanced at the display: Brendan. He'd insisted they exchange phone numbers and e-mail addresses before they'd parted that morning.

"Hello?"

"Hey, sweetheart. How'd your meeting go?"

"It just ended. I think I am going to join. I really like the church."

"Guess I'll have to check it out."

She almost dropped the phone. What did that mean? *Don't read too much into it, Lynne.* "You're welcome to come with me anytime."

"It's a date this Sunday." He shifted gears. "Do you have plans for dinner?"

"No. I was just going to make a meat loaf." She was still back on the "date this Sunday" line. "Ah, would you like to come over?"

"That would be great. I can't get home before six. I'll be over as soon as I feed Cedar."

"All right. See you then."

"I miss you. I haven't been able to think of anything but you all day."

She stopped dead. "Oh, Brendan. I feel the same way." She lowered her voice. "Hurry home so I can show you how much I missed you." Had she really just said that?

There was a moment of silence on the other end of the connection. Then he spoke again, his voice deep and rough. "I'm holding you to that, sweetheart."

At home she mixed up a pan of brownies and baked them. While they cooled, she put fresh sheets on her bed. Just in case. Then she made the meat loaf and put it in the oven with two baked potatoes. She'd steam some asparagus right before they were ready to eat.

Glancing at the clock, she saw she had time for a quick shower. Good. She pinned up her hair and jumped in the shower. When she finished, she glanced at the clock. Five-thirty. She was in fine time.

She shrugged into her robe and began to take down her hair—and froze as the doorbell rang. Rats. Who could that be? Brendan wasn't due home yet.

But when she went to the door, Feather already stood there, her tail beating a mad rhythm.

She pulled the door open. "You're early!" Then she stopped and looked around. "Where's Cedar?"

"I got away quicker than expected," Brendan said.

"He's already been fed." He shut the door and pulled her to him. "Come here."

As he slid his arms around her, plastering her against his body, she shuddered with raw need. How could he do that? One minute she was fine, the next she felt as if she were going to evaporate in a cloud of steam.

"Kiss me." She wound her arms around his neck, lifting her face to his.

After a moment, though, it was clear that Feather wasn't going to let herself be excluded. With a laugh, Brendan released Lynne and knelt to snuggle his retired guide. Finally he rose and they walked together into the kitchen where he kenneled her.

He turned then and took Lynne's hand. They walked back into the living room and he immediately pulled Lynne into his arms again. But soon he drew back. "What are you wearing?" His hands were already on the belt of her terry cloth robe, pulling it open and sliding inside to caress her bare curves.

"Brendan! We're in the living room!"

"So? Are the curtains closed?"

"Yes, but—"

"But nothing." He began to kiss her again, while his hands roamed over her, stroking and teasing, brushing repeatedly over her nipples with his thumbs until they were tight little peaks and electric sensation shot straight from her breasts to her womb with each touch. She writhed against him, but he only backed her against the wall and continued to stroke her, his hand sliding down the flat plane of her soft belly to brush the tight curls at the vee of her legs.

He shifted one knee against her, pressing until she widened her stance, and she moaned aloud as his warm hand probed deep between her legs, sliding along the tender seam, gently opening her and spreading the slick moisture he found there.

She let her head drop back against the wall and her body sagged in surrender as he bent his head to suckle her. Then she moaned again as she felt the advance of one long finger inside her, slipping in, slipping out, rubbing the throbbing bud that he uncovered at the apex of her thighs.

"Brendan," she gasped. "I can't—I can't—"

"You can," he said with determination, sliding a second finger into her. He rotated the pad of his thumb against her again and she clenched her teeth together to prevent the scream that wanted to escape. And then he touched her again and the world exploded, her body heaving and buckling against him as he ruthlessly drove her over the edge with his hand, prolonging her responses until she quivered with aftershocks. Gently he withdrew his hand, and the simple action made her briefly jerk against him again.

"Wow," she murmured. "If that's how you always come through the door, I'm going to need to take more vitamins."

He laughed, hugging her against him. "Let's make it a habit."

As she rested against him, she realized that while she might be relaxed, he was far from it. And when she slipped her hand down to cradle the bulge at the front of his trousers, he said, "Maybe we should find a bed."

"Or not." Before he could move, she dropped to her knees before him.

"What are you doing?" It was rhetorical, his voice deep with arousal and anticipation.

Slowly she unbuckled his belt, unzipped his pants and spread the fabric wide. He wore blue-and-white-striped boxers beneath, and she slipped one hand into the front opening, wrapping her fingers firmly around him and gently beginning to stroke the taut column of flesh she found.

"Lynne," he said in a guttural voice above her head, "you're going to kill me."

She smiled as she withdrew her hand and tugged the boxers out and down. "I hope not." He was fully aroused, and as he fell free, she leaned forward and caught the very tip of him with her lips. His back arched and his hands curled into fists for a moment, and then he bent and hauled her to her feet. In one smooth move, he lifted her and braced her against the door, then guided himself to her.

There was one breathless moment where she felt that the world was suspended, that everything around her was balanced on a knife-edge of desire—

—and then he took her hips in his big hands and

pulled her firmly down, thrusting forward in one long, smooth stroke until he was lodged deep inside her receptive channel. Bracing his arms against the wall on either side of her head, he began to move steadily, his buttocks flexing as he pushed into her again and again.

She wrapped her legs around his waist, pleasure so intense that she was barely able to form conscious thought. She felt a fist of need drawing tight, deep in her belly. Her arousal was fueled by her awareness of his rising excitement, and as he surged against her in the final moment of his own satisfaction, her body hurled her into climax as well. She bucked and writhed, the wall hard at her back and Brendan hard within her, until both of them were panting.

Brendan began to chuckle. "My knees feel like overcooked spaghetti. Can you walk?"

"I'm not sure." She wasn't kidding.

Slowly he lifted her off him and lowered her until her feet touched the floor. He held her hips until she locked her knees. She started to laugh then. "We need to get horizontal before we fall down."

"Good plan." He stepped out of his pants and shoes, tore off his shirt and socks, and then, gloriously naked, bent and lifted her into his arms.

"What are you doing?" she gasped.

"Give me directions."

"But I'm too heavy. Put me down."

"Directions," he said again, "or we're not going to get to a bed."

"Two steps forward and turn right!"

Eight

The next two weeks were the happiest days Lynne was sure she'd ever known in her life. She and Brendan ate dinner, cared for the dogs and spent every night together, usually in her apartment. The weekend following the first night they'd made love, Brendan came running with her.

Neither of them was exactly sure how well it was going to work. Brendan still ran on a treadmill but he hadn't jogged outside since his sighted days. But he told her there was another guide dog user in one of his online groups who had run the New York Marathon with her husband. They used a sighted-guide technique, although it was different from the typical right-hand-to-left-elbow position for walking.

So after consultation with the woman, they set out one morning for the long, straight roads that ran through the battlefield. Because of the huge volume of tourist traffic in the summer, the roads were kept in good repair. But in mid-December, there was next to no traffic.

They walked out to the battlefield to warm up, and stretched. It felt odd not to have Cedar, but the guide dog school that had trained him had given him strict warnings about not running with his dog. It was too easy to overheat a dog who was already wearing a harness, and too dangerous. He had no wish to circumvent the school's dictates on such an important issue. It was, he told her, a little different than letting the dog claim a spot on one piece of furniture.

Brendan produced a wide cotton band he'd gotten for their purpose, and they tethered themselves loosely together, her left wrist to his right.

Since each of them needed to be able to establish a steady breathing pattern, they worked out a system of non-verbal cues. He ran slightly ahead of her so that he could respond to tugs on his wrist. Her job was to cue him as well as to be sure there were no potholes or uneven spots in the road surface, and to be sure he was out of the path of oncoming vehicles.

"That was amazing!" He sounded utterly jubilant as they slowed to a walk and regained enough wind to speak again. He grabbed her with his free right arm and hauled her against him, seeking her lips. "Thank you so much. I never expected to be able to do that again."

"We can make it a regular habit," she told him when he released her. "Although from the sound of things, it might get tricky to find a safe time to run during tourist season."

"Probably. These roads get unbelievably congested." He nodded as they walked briskly back in the direction of their building. "You haven't really lived in Gettysburg until you've been here when the tourists are. It's like a plague of locusts."

"It will be interesting. I've never lived anywhere that was such a distinct tourist attraction." She couldn't wait to experience the summer season. It would mean that she'd been here long enough to really put down roots, and she'd feel more as if she really belonged in the community and less as if she were still on a long-term visit.

She awoke in the middle of the night that night, realizing he was awake, also, though he hadn't spoken. It was still a thrill to fall asleep in his arms and awake the same way. She supposed one day that would change, although she couldn't imagine it, she decided, basking in the bone-deep contentment that had infused her.

He lay on his back with her snuggled into the crook of his arm, one of her legs twined with his.

With his free hand, he idly wound a lock of her hair around and around.

"Brendan?"

"Hey."

"What are you doing?"

He abandoned her hair and reached over to tilt her face up to his for a leisurely kiss. "I was just lying here thinking about how lucky I am to have met you."

Her heart expanded a little more at the tender words. "It's a mutual feeling."

There was a comfortable silence. Then he said, "We never finished a conversation we started a couple of weeks ago."

"What conversation?" She was sleepy, sated and supremely comfortable.

Beneath her cheek his chest moved up and down as he laughed. "At the risk of being tacky by bringing up another woman's name while we're in bed together, we were talking about Kendra."

"Oh." She considered it. "Tacky, but I'm listening."

"I'd really like to tell you about her." His voice had grown serious.

She lifted her hand and caressed his cheek. "Of course."

"She was great after the accident. Very supportive, very determined not to let me sink into a pit of self-pity. She's actually the one who suggested I get a dog."

"Okay. Maybe I like her after all."

He smiled and tugged on her hair. "I still cared for

her but at the time I was totally immersed in myself. All I could think about was how my life had changed."

"Understandable."

"Maybe. Anyway, after about six months, I told her I couldn't marry her. I had this dumb idea that now that I had such big physical challenges to live with, I couldn't be the kind of husband she deserved."

"That was remarkably stupid."

He winced. "I know. I really hurt her. The one thing she asked me to promise her was that I'd go to counseling after we broke up. So I did. The psychologist I saw had also lost his vision in his twenties, and he was a big help in getting me to move past the 'why me?' stage and start living my life again. I got on the list for a dog and about six months later, I was matched with Feather."

"So why didn't you get together with Kendra again?" She lay back down in the circle of his arm. "Not that I'm complaining."

He smiled. "I felt guilty for ending it so badly, for a long time. And then I got to thinking that maybe I could fix it." He rubbed her hair absently between his fingers as he spoke. "Looking back, I think it was more the familiarity of the known relationship than anything, but I decided I wanted her back."

She tensed. She knew it, but she couldn't help it. Brendan hesitated, but then he simply went on with his story. "She was still living in the same condo she'd been in, and I just showed up there one day. I rang the bell—and some guy I didn't recognize answered the door. As soon as he saw me, he yelled for Kendra. Turns out she'd just gotten married."

"Oh. Bad timing."

"Yeah. I felt like an idiot. For a long time, I thought I still loved her. I was mad at myself for losing her, and mad at her for giving up on me, even though I know that's not rational since I was the one who pushed her away."

"Feelings aren't always rational."

"When I saw her the other day, it actually felt good to realize I didn't care for her anymore. I didn't resent her and I didn't want her." He tightened her arm, bringing her closer and kissing her temple. "I had moved on. I had met you."

A bubble of happiness expanded within her, threatening to float her right up to the ceiling.

"I never felt this way about anyone," he said. "I thought I loved Kendra, but I never felt about her the way I feel about you. I love you, Lynne."

The happiness turned to apprehension, though, as she remembered that she had yet to share her own secret. She had to tell him who she'd been. She couldn't imagine that it would matter, but…it wasn't the kind of secret she should be keeping from the man she wanted to spend the rest of her life with. And she *did*.

"Sweetheart?" He shifted her to her back, looming over her in the darkness, a large silhouette with shoulders that blocked what little light there was. "What are you thinking?"

"Make love to me," she said. She had to think about how to explain why she'd kept such a secret, before she just blurted it out. Deliberately she raised her knee where it was snuggled between his legs and rubbed it lightly back and forth, feeling him shudder as his sensitive flesh was stimulated, and when he moved to cradle himself between her legs, she immediately began to rock against him. His shaft was growing steadily, filling, throbbing and hot against her, and when he arched back and she felt the smooth head probing her tender opening, a spear of arousal went through her. She placed her feet flat on the bed and pushed up and he sucked in a startled breath as her action pushed him deeply within her.

He cupped her bottom in his big hands, tilting her up to receive his steady strokes, and as she felt the sweet surge of desire preparing to break over her head, she clutched at him, crossing her ankles behind his back to hold him deep and tight. *I love you, too,* she thought, but she couldn't say it aloud until she'd been honest with him. *I love you, too.*

They put up a Christmas tree in her apartment one Friday evening. Brendan couldn't be bothered with decorating his own apartment.

"It's not that I don't like Christmas," he told her. "But I can't see any of it, and it's a hassle to get out a bunch of stuff and then have to put it all away again. I'll be happy to help you, though."

"All right," she said, "but you at least have to let me put a wreath on your door. And help me decorate my place."

"I'll play Christmas CDs and eat cookies."

"Such a selfless volunteer."

He laughed, pleased that she wanted him to share preparations for the season. "It's a deal."

They took her SUV out to a local fast food place that had set up a Christmas tree lot. Wandering through the rows of trees, Brendan squeezed her hand through the mittens she wore. It had gotten steadily colder since they'd run the previous week, and snow was predicted for the weekend. "This is great," he said, inhaling deeply of the frosty air redolent with the scent of pine. "Brings back good memories from my childhood. My family always used to go out and cut down our tree together."

"That sounds nice." She was a little wistful. "We always had an artificial tree. My mother said it was too difficult for a single woman and two little girls to put up a real tree."

"So now you put up a real tree of your own," he said.

"So does my sister. I do it just because it's fun. She also does it because she's determined to give her children a real Christmas holiday."

"You didn't feel like you had a real one as a child?"

She shook her head. "Mother never spent much

time doing anything beyond what was necessary for CeCe and me. Don't get me wrong—she's not a bad person. But she was too absorbed in her hurt and anger at my father to focus on us."

"Do you remember them ever being together?"

"Not really. I have a few vague memories of him playing with us, but no specific ones of my whole family together. He came back for about a year after he divorced the second wife, but by the time I was nine he had left again. Then he had three more wives during my teens and early twenties, and now there's number six, the one he's just about to marry."

He was a little stunned to think of what her childhood must have been like. "He must really like alimony."

That startled a laugh out of her, and she leaned her head against him for a sweet moment before they told the sales attendant which tree they'd selected.

Back at the apartment, he helped her carry the tree upstairs and set it up in her living room. Since she had him to help, she told him, she could get a bigger tree than she normally did. He liked the way she assumed he could do most things unless he told her differently. He hadn't helped with this particular part of the Christmas ritual since he'd lost his sight, and he found it deeply satisfying to be more than just a bystander. And he was even happier to get the damned tree up the steps without breaking either of their necks.

She had delicate wooden snowflakes from Germany that felt fragile beneath his hands, a variety of balls and other ornaments that she told him were mostly red, silver and green, fluffy-feeling garland and a collection of Waterford crystal ornaments from Ireland. "My father has given CeCe and me one each year since we were born," she said, putting a smooth, cool piece of glass into his hand.

Exploring it, he realized that it was an angel, and it felt as if there was writing etched into one side. "What does this say?"

"Baby's first Christmas, with my name and birth-date. They all have my initials and the year on them."

"A nice tradition," he pronounced. "We all have Christmas stockings made by my mother. And a lot of the tree ornaments were made by her at one time or another. If there's a kind of needlework she can't do, I don't know what it is."

"I think it would be lovely to have things like that."

"Sorry, but I don't do needlework," he said, making her laugh.

When they were done, he reached for her and drew her close, feeling the rush of pleasure he always got when her long, slim curves settled against him. "Thank you for making me do this. It feels like we're creating some traditions."

She kissed his jaw. "I like the sound of that. Traditions."

"Things we'll do every year," he clarified, wanting

to be sure she understood how important she was to his life. Funny, but in just under two months, she'd become as necessary to him as…as breathing.

He felt her take a deep breath. "My sister has invited me to spend Christmas with her," she said, "but I haven't answered her yet."

Hearing the question she hadn't voiced, he said, "I guess we'd better talk about how to handle the holiday. I want to meet your family—"

"And I want you to meet them. Actually, CeCe has threatened to withhold my presents unless I bring you along for Christmas dinner."

He chuckled. "I want to introduce you to my family, too, but why don't we make our plans first and then I can explain to my mother when we'll be there."

"It would be nice to spend Christmas Eve here," she said. "And attend my own church for the first time."

"That would be nice," he said. "Church should be over by nine or so. Would you want to drive to your sister's after that?"

She shook her head. "I'd rather spend Christmas Eve right here with just the dogs and us. We can get up early in the morning and drive to CeCe's."

"And then head for my family's house sometime in the afternoon?"

"Sounds like a plan." He could hear amusement in her voice. "Although we might not fit into our clothing if we eat Christmas dinner at both places."

"I'll risk it if you will." He dropped his head,

kissing a line down the sensitive column of her neck until he could nuzzle the hollow above her collarbone. "Are we done with the tree? Because I have a present I want to give you."

She laughed, sliding her hand down the front of his body to explore the growing shape of his arousal. "I can't wait. Can I have it right now?"

Brendan's office Christmas party was held on the third Saturday of December at a local country club. Lynne was thrilled that Brendan wanted her to attend with him and meet his friends and co-workers. He'd already been to church with her twice and they'd met a number of people there. It was an intimate feeling to know that others regarded them as a couple.

Still, this party made her horribly nervous. She wanted to look good for Brendan, even though he couldn't visually appreciate it. The fact that those who knew him would be examining her was reason enough for her to want to do her best for Brendan.

But dressing up, wearing makeup and doing her hair, brought nerves and fear back to the surface. She felt like she had in the first weeks after she'd quit modeling. She'd come home to live for a while until she could find a place of her own. Every time she left the house, she had felt like a field mouse venturing out of hiding, exposing itself to predators. She'd been certain someone would figure out that she'd been a sort of celebrity, terrified someone would recognize her face.

But as time wore on, she was struck by one utterly astonishing fact. Most people were far too wrapped up in their own lives and concerns to think much about the new face they'd just met. Every once in a while, someone would look puzzled, as Brendan's friend Brink had, and ask if they'd met before. Not a single person had ever made the connection.

She would tell Brendan soon, she promised herself. Before Christmas. Then they could start the new year with nothing hidden, nothing standing unspoken between them. Although, really, she was beginning to wonder if she was being paranoid, assuming someone was going to recognize her.

It was the coloring, she had concluded months ago. Without makeup, her eyes were unremarkable and the facial emphasis was on her bone structure and porcelain skin. But with makeup...with the right makeup her eyes became dark, sultry pools. When she painted her lips in the bold colors that the red hair she'd had demanded, her mouth became pouty and eye catching. And then there had been that hair, a bright, curly explosion of attention-grabbing proportions. Without the hair, she was a whole new person.

It had just taken her a while to relax and realize it.

But now she had a quandary. She needed to dress up for the party. Dressing up meant wearing some makeup, making some effort. And taking the chance that her face might trigger someone's memory.

Still, she didn't feel she had a choice. She couldn't dress down. Brendan had told her that after Brink's father retired in another year, Brink had offered him partnership in the firm. It was a wonderful opportunity for him, and she needed to support that.

So she did what she could to camouflage herself. As A'Lynne, no last name needed, she'd nearly always worn the red hair loose and flowing to show off the curl. For the party, she pulled it up into a smooth, severe French twist.

She'd usually worn black, as well, since the hair precluded a number of other colors. Brendan was wearing a tux so she needed to wear something long. She still had some striking gowns, but instead she drove an hour to her sister's house one day and borrowed a deceptively simple pine-green velvet gown. It was sleeveless and fitted, with a draped cowl neckline, but it plunged to the waist in the back. She knew the texture and the cut would appeal to Brendan's sense of touch, and it certainly drew attention away from her face.

Her face. There was little she could do except go light with the application of color. She chose subdued earth tones rather than the brassy pinks and plums they'd used on her for photo shoots, did the best she could to make herself look attractive and classy without making her face unforgettable and promised herself she was not going to agonize about it all night. Not much, anyway.

When he crossed the hall and knocked on her door, Brendan looked handsome and imposing in a severe black tux with a black shirt and tie. He didn't have Cedar with him. He'd debated about bringing him, he told her, but had finally decided to let his guide relax at home, since they would largely be sitting at a dining table.

Brink and his date picked them up. The party would be attended by several law firms in the area. Each firm's dinners were small affairs, held either in private rooms at the country club or elsewhere around town. But after dinner, there was a dance in the club's elegant ballroom, to which all the guests had tickets regardless of where their dinner party had been held.

As Brink pulled into their parking lot, Brendan said to her, "You do realize it will be your job to let me know if I drop food on my lapels."

"Oooh," she said as he helped her into the back seat of Brink's Mercedes, "I guess that gives you some incentive to be nice to me."

He walked around the car, folded his cane, took his place beside her and slammed the door. While Brink was seating Amanda, Brendan leaned over and growled, "I intend to be very, very nice to you later, sweetheart."

"I can't wait," she purred, sliding one finger upward from his knee along his muscled thigh.

"Ah-ah-ah." He grabbed her hand and linked their fingers. "Unless you want to embarrass us both, that's a really bad idea. It's only a short ride to the country club."

Dinner itself was pleasant. They were seated at a table with Brink and Amanda, and the two men's office assistants and their husbands.

The other two women gave them a run-down of who was who in the room, with commentary from Brink, who seemed to be a one-man talk show. She was glad, actually, since it meant she didn't have to talk much and people's attention was focused elsewhere.

After dessert, the tables were cleared and the live band began to play. It was an excellent group and as the notes of the first slow song began, he rose and took her hand. "Dance with me."

It was heaven. She hadn't known him long enough to take being in his arms for granted. And she loved to dance. Brendan was a strong partner and with a minimum of direction from her to keep them from plowing into other couples, they moved extremely well together.

During one break from the music, he asked Brink a low question, and when his friend answered, Brendan's head swiveled to the left. After a brief nod, Brendan turned to her and said, "I want to introduce you to Mr. Brinkmen, Sr. His own father opened this firm and he took it over when Brink's grandfather retired. Now he's looking at Brink to do the same thing."

"And then you will become a partner?"

Brendan nodded. "Brinkmen & Reilly, Attorneys-at-Law. Has a pleasant ring, don't you think?"

She laughed. "I do."

His voice deepened. "Sort of like Mr. & Mrs. Brendan Reilly also has a nice ring to it. Even better, Lynne Reilly. I like that particularly well."

Was he asking her to marry him? Completely thrown, she said the first thing that came into her head. "I love it, but since no one named Reilly has asked me to marry him, this is all hypothetical."

Brendan laughed so hard people around them turned to look. "Trust you to cut straight to the heart of the matter." He slid his hands up her arms to cup her elbows. "Lynne, I didn't intend to do this tonight. I haven't bought a ring yet. But since we seem to be standing here tiptoeing around the most important topic we might ever discuss together… will you marry me?"

Her head was reeling. She had to remind herself to breathe. "Brendan—are you sure? Wait! I didn't mean that."

He laughed again. "I'd take a one-word answer right about now."

"Yes," she said hastily. "Oh, yes!"

Unaware, and probably uncaring of the curious stares of those around them who sensed something was up, Brendan slid his arms around her and kissed her, bending her backward so that she was clinging to his strong neck, depending on him to support her.

When he raised his head, he said, "Hey, everybody, this beautiful lady has just agreed to marry me."

Around them, clapping, whistles and cheers erupted.

"Way to go, buddy!" Brink was there slapping Brendan on the back, while one of the office assistants threw her arms around Lynne.

"Congratulations, dear. Brendan is one of the finest young men I know."

She opened her mouth to respond, but her mobile phone, in her small evening bag on the table, began to play its distinctive tune. Startled, she said, "Oh! That's my phone. Excuse me."

Concern filled her even before she flipped open the top and spoke. She really kept the phone with her only for family emergencies, or so that her mother could reach her if needed. She honestly couldn't even remember the last time it had rung since she'd moved to Gettysburg.

"Hello?"

"Lynnie?" It was CeCe, and Lynne immediately realized she was crying.

"Cees, what's wrong?" She felt her stomach drop as if she were in a plane that had just hit an air pocket. "Are you okay?"

"I'm okay," CeCe said, "but Lynnie, Daddy's in the hospital. Can you come?"

"Of course." Immediately she reached for a napkin and began to scribble down directions. "What happened?"

CeCe cried harder. "He went jogging with the new wife-to-be. Apparently she's a serious marathoner and they ran ten miles—and Daddy collapsed. They think he might have had a heart attack."

"Ten miles!" Their father was in excellent shape, but— "Didn't he tell her he's never run more than three or four in his life?"

"You know Daddy," CeCe said, her voice slightly calmer. "He'd die before he'd admit he wasn't as strong and fit as a younger man."

There was a sudden silence as she realized what she'd just said, and then she began to cry again. "Can you come right away, Lynne?"

"Of course."

Without hesitation, Lynne agreed and went to tell Brendan what had happened, disappointed and distressed at the dramatic turn of events. How could the best moment of her life suddenly become the worst?

Nine

On Monday morning Lynne called Brendan at the office. She'd kept in close touch since she'd rushed out of town Saturday evening to be with her father. As it turned out, he had, indeed, had a mild heart attack.

Lynne had been overwhelmed with concern after speaking with her sister, frantic to get on the road, and Brink had driven them home immediately. There was no question of Brendan going; he needed to care for the dogs.

She'd been a whirlwind back at the building. He was pretty sure she'd changed, packed and rushed out the door in under five minutes.

"Good morning," he said in response to her greeting. "How's your dad today?"

"Doing much better." There was a wry note in her voice. "He's getting boatloads of loving attention from Alison, the newest attraction. He might have faked getting sick before if he'd realized how much attention he'd get. Kidding," she added with a laugh, "I think."

They talked for a few more minutes about her family, and Brendan reassured her that the dogs were well.

"I miss you," he said. "Sleeping alone has no appeal anymore."

"I miss you, too," she said. "Daddy's being discharged this afternoon, so once he's back in his apartment with Alison to take care of him, I'll head home."

"I'll look forward to it," he said. And he would. He'd spent two hours at the jeweler's down the street from the office today, selecting a ring. He'd taken his office assistant with him and he hoped he'd chosen a ring that Lynne would treasure. He'd get some flowers on the way home, and tonight they could make their engagement official.

After a few more minutes they hung up and he turned his attention back to the brief on which he was working. He'd been immersed in it for thirty minutes when he noted Brink returning from the court appearance he'd had in the morning.

He'd already tuned the distraction out and gotten back to work when his office door burst open.

"I finally figured it out," Brink crowed. "You sly dog."

"Good morning to you, too. Figured what out?"

"You know. Lynne."

"What the hell are you talking about?" He finally stopped the screen reader and gave Brink his attention. "Figured what out?"

"You know…Lynne. Who she really is."

"Oh, you did, huh?" His tone was dry. "Wanna share this revelation? I'm sure it'll be good for a laugh."

There was an odd pause, making him wish he could still read his buddy's expression. "You're joking. Right? She's A'Lynne. From *Sports Illustrated*."

"Allan who?"

"No, not Allan. Ah-LIN, and not a guy. A supermodel—only one name. She was on the cover of *Sports Illustrated*'s swimsuit edition a couple of years ago. You knew," Brink asserted. "You're just jerking my chain."

"No," he said carefully, "I am not kidding. You really believe this model Lynne resembles is her?"

Brendan heard the thud of a magazine on his desk. "I keep all the old *SI* swimsuit editions. It's the same woman. I even asked Dad and he agreed."

He was silent for a moment. Finally he said, "You're crazy. What makes you think it's her?"

"I almost missed it. She looks different now. She used to have this wild, curly red hair. It was kind of her trademark. And she was tanned and of course, wearing a boatload of makeup. But I am telling you, Brendan, it's definitely the same face. Bone structure, the shape of her eyes and lips… And the body matches. Tall and slender, although she looks a lot skinnier in the magazine. Think about it," Brink urged. "The name's similar, just Lynne with an extra *A*-apostrophe. Are you telling me you don't know this?"

"She's never mentioned it, *if* it's even true." He feigned unconcern, though his heart was racing. "I'll run it by her tonight. I imagine it'll give her a good chuckle. But, thanks. It's pretty flattering, I guess, that you mistook my girlfriend—my fiancée now—for a supermodel."

There was silence in the wake of his words. Finally Brink said, "Okay. Must be my mistake. She'll think it's an amazing coincidence." He sounded relieved when his assistant called from behind him that he had a phone call. "I'll talk to you later, man."

She had missed Brendan more than she'd ever thought possible. As she unlocked her door and let herself in that evening, she could hardly wait to drop her bags and rush across the hall into his arms.

But she didn't get the chance. As she came out of her bedroom, the front door opened and Brendan strode in.

"Hello!" she said. "I was just coming to you." She crossed the room and wound her arms around his neck to kiss him—

And he stepped away.

Too shocked to react, she just stood there.

Brendan tossed a magazine on the table beside the door. "Explain this."

Automatically she glanced down at the magazine. And froze.

There she was, clad in sand, a deep tan and an extremely skimpy azure bikini, on the cover of *Sports Illustrated*. It was one of the most coveted assignments in the world—and she could still remember how unhappy she'd been at that time. Separated from her family, distressed by the shallow pleasures so many of her friends chose to pursue, deeply depressed by the ending of her relationship with Jeremy, with whom she'd really thought she'd found love... She didn't even know what to say. "Where did you get this?"

"It must have been amusing for you," Brendan said furiously, "hanging with someone who would never be able to figure out who you were."

"It wasn't amusing! It was...wonderful." She was bewildered by the depths of his anger. "I know I should have told you before, but—"

"Gee, you think?" His heavy sarcasm cut across her explanation. "Brink thinks I'm an idiot. And I guess I am. I expected honesty from the woman I cared for—"

"I never lied to you!"

"Omission is a form of lying," he retorted. "You deceived me. Deliberately."

"It wasn't deliberate." But she had known it was wrong to keep the information from him. Guilt bit deep, and defiance colored her response. "When we met, I owed you nothing other than my name. And Lynne Devane *is* my real name." She was fighting tears of distress and of rising anger at his accusations. "And then as we started getting to know each other, I just…I enjoyed knowing you liked me for me, not because it was cool to be with someone *famous.*"

"That sounds nice," he said, "but it still doesn't explain why you didn't tell me. *I asked you to marry me!* Didn't it occur to you that perhaps I ought to know what I was really getting?"

He was shouting by the time he finished, and she shrank back, folding her arms and hugging herself, holding herself together as the dreams she'd built since she'd met him began to drift away like wisps of smoke. "You think you know it all, Mr. Perfect," she said, a sob catching her voice. "But let me tell you what the life of a top model is like. You can't leave your room without people chasing you around asking questions and taking pictures. You never know if the people you meet are genuine or if they only want to get close to you because they think some glamour might rub off on them. Your manager fusses about every bite you put in your mouth and you have to fight to keep from doing what three-quarters of your co-workers do, which is eat like fools and then purge, or else starve themselves because they're convinced they're fat. You're offered drugs and asked on dates by creeps who assume that because you're an international celebrity you'll have sex with them. And sometimes one of them is nice to you, and sweet, and gentle and you really think maybe this one is different—" she had to swallow another sob "—and then you find out he's not different at all, that he just wants you because you increase his own status." She poked him in the chest with a finger. "Don't you *ever* dare to judge my reasons for trying to keep a low profile."

She slid past him, careful not to touch him, and reached for the doorknob. Then she turned back to him and said, "I thought you were different. I thought you loved me for *who* I was, not *what* I was."

"I did!"

"You go right ahead and tell yourself that. You're as bad as Jeremy in a different way. He wanted me for what I was. You *don't* want me for the same reason. Now get out."

"Lynne—"

"Get out!"

She couldn't stop crying. All night, she sobbed, on and off, until at daybreak she finally quit trying to sleep and got up. She paced around her apartment, Feather following anxiously behind.

At seven-thirty, reality struck her with the force of a blow. It was over. There was no going back from the angry words she and Brendan had exchanged last night. What was she going to do? How could she stand to live across the hall from him, see him casually again and again? How could she bear knowing what he thought of her?

The answer to the final question was clear: she couldn't bear it. At least, not if she had to be confronted with his scorn. That, she could do something about.

She rushed back to her room and hauled out a bigger suitcase than the bag she'd taken when her father was ill, haphazardly tossing in a variety of clothing items that would get her through a week or so. She would contact the Realtor from whom she'd rented the place and see about a sublet. She could stay with CeCe for a few more days while she figured out what on earth she was going to do next. Clearly she couldn't stay in Gettysburg.

She should have been warned when she learned that his engagement hadn't been broken off for the reasons she'd assumed. Instead of being dumped, Brendan was actually the dumper—and for a stupid presumption that he wasn't good enough for a sighted wife. He said he'd gotten over it and she'd believed him.

But he'd made another stupid presumption about her "motives" for getting involved with him, a presumption that showed her his uncertainties still existed. Like the fact that he couldn't see had actually had a single thing to do with her reasons for not telling him about her past career. If he'd been sighted and hadn't figured it out, she would have done exactly the same thing. Maybe it *was* deception but it hadn't been malicious.

She loved him, dammit! Rage and despair lent impetus to her actions, and the suitcase was filled in mere moments. Slamming the lid shut, she grabbed the toiletries case that she hadn't even unpacked yet. She was halfway to the door before she realized she couldn't just leave Feather behind.

And she couldn't take her along, she realized with a heavy heart. Feather wasn't hers.

Sad and angry, she sank down onto the edge of the couch and bent to wrap her arms around the old dog. Fondling her ears, she said, "I'm sorry, girl. You know I'll always love you. But I have to go."

She rubbed the silky edge of Feather's ears, tears streaming down her face. The only thing she could do was leave the door unlocked and call Brendan to come over and get her after she was gone.

He heard her apartment door close and her footsteps recede down the hall, but he was too angry to talk to her again for a while.

And hurt. He could admit that. She hadn't trusted him. He'd been willing, even eager, to give her his heart, and she hadn't felt the same way. If she had, she would have confided in him weeks ago.

How many weeks ago? You haven't even known her eight weeks yet.

And in that short period of time, he'd fallen deeply in love. For someone who'd lived the life he now realized she had been immersed in, she was remarkably unassuming. Her tastes were simple, her desires few. She was even tempered rather than arrogant, loving and tenderhearted rather than expecting adulation.

Good God. He'd had a supermodel taking care of his dog. It was hard to even comprehend. Although he'd made his peace with his loss of sight years ago, every once in a while he bitterly regretted not being able to see. This was one of those times. Perhaps if he could see Lynne, compare her to that magazine—

Why? So you'd have proof that she was someone different?

Different on the surface, perhaps, but the very fact that she'd walked away from that lifestyle and chosen this—*chosen him*—spoke volumes about her character.

The telephone rang. He leaped for it, willing it to be her. "Hello?"

"Brendan. You need to go across the hall and get Feather. I left my door unlocked. Her toys and lead and bowl are in a bag on the counter."

"Lynne, you don't have to give her back—"

"I'm not going to be living there anymore. I'm sorry, but I won't be able to take care of her for you." She rushed on before he could react. "I've enjoyed her. Thank you for that. Goodbye."

And in another instant there was a dial tone in his

ear. She'd left! She'd left for good. Moved out. Well, obviously she hadn't moved out yet, but she intended to.

He sank onto the couch with his head in his hands, anger suddenly forgotten as the finality in her stricken tone sank in.

Dear God, what had he done?

He left nine messages on her mobile phone in the first two days, but she never called him back. He was frantic, wondering if her father's health had taken a turn for the worse or if the only reason she was staying away was because she was so hurt.

Tuesday dragged by, then Wednesday and Thursday. By Friday he was wondering if she ever planned to return. The weekend passed in a dull haze of sadness. And anger—anger at himself. He knew better than to let a knee-jerk reaction dictate his behavior. He'd been trained to stop and think things through.

How could he have been so stupid?

I thought you loved me for who I was, not what I was.

Funny how much sense that made now that he was past the initial hurt and anger he'd felt. There had to be a way to talk to her. To make her understand that he was sorry for the things he'd said. But…for an attorney who'd passed the bar exam with one of the highest scores in the state, he felt pretty clueless, because he hadn't come up with one viable idea for getting Lynne to speak to him again.

Monday evening he trudged up the stairs. He'd been home at lunch to let Feather out, but Lynne still hadn't come home. He would know the minute she arrived. All he had to do was keep an eye on his dog.

He'd never seen Feather so subdued. She'd been depressed and annoyed when he'd retired her and she'd had to deal with a new dog in the house, but now she was so different he was starting to worry in earnest. She didn't even get to her feet when he arrived home anymore. Yesterday he'd made an appointment with the vet because she'd eaten so little in the past few days he was worried about her weight.

He unlocked his door and entered his apartment. "Feather," he called. "Hey, girl. Where are you?" No sound betrayed her presence. "Feather?" He called her name four times before he heard a deep doggy sigh and the sound of her feet shuffling across the floor toward him. His heart broke a little more as her unhappiness hit him almost as a physical blow. She was a golden retriever, a breed that practically was listed in the dictionary beside the word *bounce*. But she hadn't shown any sign of vibrancy in days.

"I'm sorry, old girl." He knelt as she approached, and when her head came to rest against his chest, he massaged her silky ears. He hadn't cried since he was a child but he caught himself swallowing a lump lodged in his throat at the palpable misery his beloved old friend exuded. "I want her back, too," he whispered.

Suddenly, with energy Feather hadn't shown in

days, the dog reared back and tore away from him. He heard her nails frantically clacking across the floor to the door, and then she began to bark. Cedar followed her, less excited but interested in whatever had gotten her so worked up.

Hope rose faster than he could get to the door. Feather acted this way when Brink was around, but just maybe... He rushed after her, misjudged the distance to the door and nearly slammed into it face-first. He caught himself with a hand against the wood mere moments before his nose would have met it. There was a tremendous bang as the door trembled in its frame.

Hell! For a moment he wasn't sure whether to pray it was Brink so that Lynne didn't figure out what an ass he'd just made of himself, or whether Lynne would be kinder than Brink, who would tease him unmercifully for days.

"Brendan? Are you all right?"

It was Lynne's voice! His knees suddenly trembled as if they were about to give way, and a sweeping relief carried him along as he yanked open the door and rushed into the hallway right behind Feather. Cedar, agitated at the near accident, hovered close beside him.

"Hey." He tried for casual, but was afraid he failed miserably. "I'm fine. I'm glad you're back."

There was a taut silence. "I'm not staying," she said, and her voice was subdued. "I just came to get a few important things that I don't want to risk getting lost or damaged when the movers come." He heard her kneel, and as Feather quieted he knew she must be cuddling the dog.

"The movers?"

"They'll be here Friday."

"Friday." He felt as if the words were bouncing off the surface of his brain, incomprehensible. "This Friday?"

"Yes." He could barely hear her.

"But…you can't move," he said.

Another silence. He waited, hoping for a response, any response. But she made none.

"Please come in and see Feather." He didn't care that he probably sounded desperate. "She isn't eating well. She misses you."

Lynne knelt on the floor, rubbing Feather's silky ears, resting her forehead against the old dog's. "You be a good girl," she told her in a low voice. "No more of this picky-eater stuff. And be nice to Cedar." Her voice broke and she cleared her throat as she rose. "No, thank you," she said. "I need to get started." This would probably be the last time she would ever see Brendan, and she drank in his familiar features, wishing there was a way to go back two months and start over.

"Lynne," he said, "I'm sorry."

His head lowered and she couldn't quite read his

expression. She blinked, unsure she'd really heard him right. Sorry for what?

"I know it probably doesn't change anything now, but I want you to know that I really am sorry. I had no right to judge you without asking you why you felt it necessary to be anonymous."

She swallowed, her throat so choked that she could barely speak. "Maybe not. But I was wrong to deceive you in the first place so I apologize, too." She couldn't take another minute of polite, earnest regret, so she turned toward her door. "Goodbye, Brendan."

"Where are you going?" He was standing between her and her apartment door and he didn't budge.

"I already told you I was moving. The landlord is subletting my apartment here for the remainder of my lease." She tried to smile. "I asked him to be sure it was someone who loved dogs."

He stepped forward, and she moved to the side so that he could pass her. Instead, with the uncanny intuition she'd observed before, he reached right for her, his hands sliding down her arms to link her fingers with his. "Don't go."

"I have to." She couldn't hold back the tears.

"No," he said. "You don't." He gathered her against him and she wanted to be there too badly to struggle away.

"I do," she said. Throwing pride to the wind, she cried, "I can't stay here. I'm not strong enough to help you with Feather, to see you every day, to live across the hall from you and never be able to be with you again." She pushed out of his arms. "I appreciate your apology, I really do, and I will always wish I had done things differently, but—"

He put his arms around her again. Lowering his head, he covered her lips with his, cutting off her protests. He kissed her as he always had, exploring and devouring her, eliciting a helpless response until she raised her arms and cradled his head, kissing him back with no regard for her heart's protection.

When he finally tore his lips away from hers, it was only to transfer his mouth to her neck. "Make love with me," he said against her skin.

"No." She struggled again, desperate to get away before she completely dissolved into tears. Was he enjoying making this so difficult?

"Why not?" He was relentless. "That's exactly what it would be—making love. I love you, Lynne." His voice grew passionate. "And I know you love me. I was wrong. The woman I fell in love with is no different from the woman you've been all your life. If I've learned anything, I learned that."

She bit her lip. She wanted to believe him, wanted to let go of all the sadness and heartache of the past few days, but… "I do love you." She cleared her throat. "But, Brendan, I can't change my past. I'm always going to have been a supermodel."

"Do you still want to be one? Because if you do,

or if you decide you might like to go back, I'll support your decision."

"No!" That was one thing of which she was certain. "I just want to be a regular person with a regular life."

"Okay. We can do that." He lifted a hand and cradled her cheek, and she felt her doubts begin to slip away. "I want to make you happy, sweetheart. And I don't think you're going to be happy if you leave me."

"I don't think I am, either," she confessed. "But can you really be happy with me now that you know I'm not just the girl next door?"

"No problem." He drew her against him again, his big body warm and solid against her. "I don't want you to be the girl next door, anyway. I want you to be my wife."

Tears stung her eyes. "I want that, too. Are you sure?"

He smiled as he took her hand and drew her into his apartment. "I have something for you. I was going to wait until Christmas morning, but now I think I'd better not."

She allowed him to seat her on the couch and watched as he went to his bedroom and returned with a small package wrapped in silver and gaily tied with soft red ribbon. Her heart skipped a beat as hope rose within her.

Taking a seat beside her, he found her hand and turned it palm up, setting the small box there. "Open it."

"Now? I don't have your presents wrapped yet." She wanted to open it badly, but her hands were shaking, and she pressed the small box tightly between them.

"After the way I behaved, the only present I want is you," he said. He slid from the couch to one knee and loosely cradled her hands in his. "I already asked you to marry me once, but I'm asking again. Will you marry me?"

For the first time, she felt a glimmer of happiness return. "Oh, Brendan, are you sure?" Her throat closed on the words.

"Absolutely," he said. "There is nothing you could tell me that could make me change my mind. I already learned the hard way that having you in my life is more important than anything that could come between us."

"Does it bother you that I'm independently wealthy?" Might as well drag every skeleton out and make sure it wasn't going to fall apart at her feet later.

He snorted, and she knew her fears were needless. "You mean, is my masculinity threatened? Nah. Just as long as you can't run faster, jump higher or leap buildings in a single bound. That might put me off."

"You're in no danger." Happiness allowed her to respond in the same jesting manner. "Physical fitness was not my best subject in school. I run now to keep in shape, but there's no speed involved in the activity. And I certainly do not bound."

"That's settled, then." He squeezed her hands lightly. "So open this."

She took a deep breath. "All right." Slowly she pulled off the ribbon and carefully pried open the wrapping paper without tearing it.

"What are you doing?" Impatience rang in his tone. "Don't tell me you're a paper saver!"

"I most certainly am."

He sighed. "Wake me when you're ready to open the box."

But she'd already slipped the small jeweler's box from the square white one, and as she flipped the lid, Brendan's head snapped up.

He didn't move—and neither did she.

Finally he said, "Well?" and there was uncertainty in his voice once again.

"It's...incredible," she said in a small voice. And it was.

"You like it? I told the jeweler what I wanted and he helped me with the details."

"I love it," she said fervently. "There's a large diamond in the center with two smaller ones on each side and the whole band in studded with tiny chips. It's radiating light like I can't even describe."

He reached for the box and removed the ring, then picked up her left hand and found her ring finger. Sliding the ring into place, he asked, "How does it fit?"

"It's perfect!" She held out her hand, unable to believe she was wearing such a lovely ring.

"Good," he said. "It will match my wife. Perfect."

"I love you, too." She laughed. "Yikes. Nothing like high expectations to live up to!"

"You're not going to have any trouble." He paused, and drew her into his arms. "I love you, sweetheart. The day I fell over your boxes was the best day of my life."

She laughed, her lips skimming over his face. "Just think of the story we'll have to tell our children of how we met."

"Our children. I like the sound of that." He rose, drawing her up with him and linking her fingers with his. "We should get started."

"Telling the story?"

"No." He pulled her against him, fitting his hard frame to the softness of her yielding body. "Making the children."

"Brendan! We're not even married yet!"

"So? At the very least, we should practice. We want to be sure we get it right."

And as his hands slipped beneath her sweater, seeking the soft, warm skin beneath, she tugged his tie loose and started opening the buttons of his dress shirt. "By all means, let's make sure we get it right."

* * * * *

New York Times *bestselling author*
Linda Lael Miller
is back with a new romance featuring the
heartwarming McKettrick family from
Silhouette Special Edition.

SIERRA'S HOMECOMING
by Linda Lael Miller

On sale December 2006,
wherever books are sold.

Turn the page for a sneak preview!

Soft, smoky music poured into the room.

The next thing she knew, Sierra was in Travis's arms, close against that chest she'd admired earlier, and they were slow dancing.

Why didn't she pull away?

"Relax," he said. His breath was warm in her hair.

She giggled, more nervous than amused. What was the matter with her? She was attracted to Travis, had been from the first, and he was clearly attracted to her. They were both adults. Why not enjoy a little slow dancing in a ranch-house kitchen?

Because slow dancing led to other things. She took a step back and felt the counter flush against her lower back. Travis naturally came with her, since they were holding hands and he had one arm around her waist.

Simple physics.

Then he kissed her.

Physics again—this time, not so simple.

"Yikes," she said, when their mouths parted.

He grinned. "Nobody's ever said that after I kissed them."

She felt the heat and substance of his body pressed against hers. "It's going to happen, isn't it?" she heard herself whisper.

"Yep," Travis answered.

"But not tonight," Sierra said on a sigh.

"Probably not," Travis agreed.

"When, then?"

He chuckled, gave her a slow, nibbling kiss. "Tomorrow morning," he said. "After you drop Liam off at school."

"Isn't that…a little…soon?"

"Not soon enough," Travis answered, his voice husky. "Not nearly soon enough."

Harlequin® Historical
Historical Romantic Adventure!

Loyalty...or love?

LORD GREVILLE'S CAPTIVE
Nicola Cornick

He had previously come to Grafton Manor to be betrothed to the beautiful Lady Anne—but that promise was broken with the onset of the English Civil War. Now Lord Greville has returned as an enemy, besieging the manor and holding its lady prisoner.

His devotion to his cause is swayed by his desire for Anne—he will have the lady, and her heart.

Yet Anne has a secret that must be kept from him at all costs....

On sale December 2006.
Available wherever Harlequin books are sold.

REQUEST YOUR FREE BOOKS!

2 FREE NOVELS PLUS 2 FREE GIFTS!

Passionate, Powerful, Provocative!

YES! Please send me 2 FREE Silhouette Desire® novels and my 2 FREE gifts. After receiving them, if I don't wish to receive any more books, I can return the shipping statement marked "cancel." If I don't cancel, I will receive 6 brand-new novels every month and be billed just $3.80 per book in the U.S., or $4.47 per book in Canada, plus 25¢ shipping and handling per book and applicable taxes, if any*. That's a savings of almost 15% off the cover price! I understand that accepting the 2 free books and gifts places me under no obligation to buy anything. I can always return a shipment and cancel at any time. Even if I never buy another book from Silhouette, the two free books and gifts are mine to keep forever.

225 SDN EEXJ   326 SDN EEXU

Name	(PLEASE PRINT)
Address	Apt.
City	State/Prov.	Zip/Postal Code

Signature (if under 18, a parent or guardian must sign)

Mail to Silhouette Reader Service™:

IN U.S.A.	**IN CANADA**
P.O. Box 1867	P.O. Box 609
Buffalo, NY	Fort Erie, Ontario
14240-1867	L2A 5X3

Not valid to current Silhouette Desire subscribers.

Want to try two free books from another line?
Call 1-800-873-8635 or visit www.morefreebooks.com.

* Terms and prices subject to change without notice. NY residents add applicable sales tax. Canadian residents will be charged applicable provincial taxes and GST. This offer is limited to one order per household. All orders subject to approval. Credit or debit balances in a customer's account(s) may be offset by any other outstanding balance owed by or to the customer. Please allow 4 to 6 weeks for delivery.

SDES06

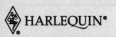

HARLEQUIN®

American ROMANCE®

IS PROUD TO PRESENT

COWBOY VET
by Pamela Britton

Jessie Monroe is the last person on earth
Rand Sheppard wants to rely on, but he needs
a veterinary technician—yesterday—and she's the
only one for hire. It turns out the woman who
destroyed his cousin's life isn't who Rand thought
she was. And now she's all he can think about!

"Pamela Britton writes the kind of
wonderfully romantic, sexy, witty romance
that readers dream of discovering
when they go into a bookstore."

—*New York Times* bestselling author
Jayne Ann Krentz

**Cowboy Vet *is available from
Harlequin American Romance in December 2006.***

www.eHarlequin.com   HARPBDEC